Richard H. Wilmer, Charles L. Norton

Jack Benson's Log

Afloat with the flag in '61

Richard H. Wilmer, Charles L. Norton

Jack Benson's Log
Afloat with the flag in '61

ISBN/EAN: 9783337090494

Printed in Europe, USA, Canada, Australia, Japan

Cover: Foto ©Andreas Hilbeck / pixelio.de

More available books at **www.hansebooks.com**

"DAVY AND I WERE PERCHED IN THE CROSSTREES."

JACK BENSON'S LOG;

OR,

AFLOAT WITH THE FLAG IN '61.

BY

CHARLES LEDYARD NORTON.

ILLUSTRATED BY GEORGE GIBBS.

BOSTON:

W. A. WILDE & COMPANY,

25 BROMFIELD STREET.

JACK BENSON'S LOG.

CONTENTS.

CHAPTER.   PAGE.

I.   A Sailor Boy's Birthright   7

II.   Secession at Rockledge   25

III. On the Danger Line   38

IV.   The Saving of " Old Ironsides "   58

V.   Massachusetts and New York to the Rescue . . .   85

VI.   Mutiny or Treason   93

VII. The " Otter's " First Prize   122

VIII. A Running Fight   138

IX.   Contraband of War   151

X.   Our First Innings   161

XI.   Contrabands as Coast Pilots   175

XII. The Slave Driver of Santee   195

XIII. " Come Aboard, Sir ! "   225

XIV. Iron Against Wood   252

XV.   Iron Against Iron   266

ILLUSTRATIONS.

PAGE.

"Davy and I were perched in the crosstrees" . . . *Frontispiece*

"Where are you going with that bag, young fellow?" . . . 42

"Old Abe was elected, you say?" 99

Getting into action off Hatteras 168

"Come aboard, sir!" 238

JACK BENSON'S LOG.

CHAPTER I.

A SAILOR BOY'S BIRTHRIGHT.

I, JOHN BENSON, a retired officer of the navy, was born in the ancient seaport town of Stony-haven in the year of grace one thousand eight hundred and forty-five, and of the independence of the United States the sixty-eighth.

Probably I am thus particular in detailing the facts of my appearance in this world from early recollections of Thanksgiving and Fast Day procla-mations as read annually from the church pulpits of my native town. My father was skipper and part owner of the fishing schooner "Molly Pitcher," which, when she was not hauled out on the ways undergoing repairs after some unusually rough treatment on the high seas, was away in pursuit of herring, or mackerel, or cod, or halibut, according to the season of the year or the de-mands of the market.

Built for the Crowninshields of Salem by "Kit"

Turner, she served her owners as a pleasure yacht until the first international sailing matches were arranged for the seasons of 1812–14, when she, refitted with a brace of long thirty-twos and sundry carronades in broadside, shipped a crew of North Shore sailormen, and won nearly every race for which she entered, whether it was running away from lumbering British men-o'-war or capturing merchant vessels of many times her own tonnage.

When I was old enough to make her acquaintance she was still stanch from stem to sternpost, and so tight that her crew used to say " she did not leak enough to keep her sweet." My grandfather was one of her crew when she took in a West Indiaman in the Bahama Channel, and as I look up from my library table I can see the old privateersman's cutlass and brass-mounted pistols hanging against the chimney-piece beside Captain Abner Shumway's sword and cocked hat.

My earliest recollection is of lying awake at night and listening to the thunder of breakers on the rocky headland that sheltered Stonyhaven Harbor and seeing my mother come in with a frightened face, shading the candle with her hand so that the light should not awaken me. Some silly boyish instinct prompted me to feign sleep, and she presently kissed me softly and went out.

The revolving light on the cape was distant only a short mile from my father's house, and was visible from the tiny square window of my little sleeping-room. From early infancy I had habitually fallen asleep watching the red square of reflected light that appeared and re-appeared on the wall at the foot of my bed with such mechanical regularity that to watch it was to become drowsy and finally to drop off into unconsciousness. How many times since then, when harassed by wakefulness, have I longed for that sleep-compelling light from Stonyhaven Head!

But on the night in question the red square was blurred, and indistinct, and irregular by intervening sheets of rain and scud. It would not send me to sleep as usual, and presently, through the roar of the tempest, there came the dull sound of a distant gun, and then, after a long pause, it was repeated, and I, frightened, sat up in bed and called my mother. For, little as I was, I was a sailorman's boy and knew that minute guns meant a ship in distress.

She came in, looking pale and watchworn, for, as she said, it was now near dawn, and she had not closed her eyes since it came on to blow just after the tide turned at midnight. I dressed hastily and found her in the sitting-room, with a bright

fire in the kitchen beyond; and presently the
windows on the easterly side of the house became
whitish gray instead of black, and we knew that
the horror of thick darkness was passing away.
And then my mother made coffee and we both had
something to eat, and then, for by that time it was
light enough to see houses across the street, she
began putting on her storm wraps, and I knew that
she was going down to the breakwater to learn if
there was any news of the " Molly Pitcher."

I sat half tearfully watching her, for I had
always been left at home on such occasions before,
but now, being comparatively big, I took a sudden
resolve, fetched my red-topped boots, the pride of
my boyish heart, from the closet, and began putting
them on.

"Where are you going, Johnny?" asked my
mother.

"Going with you to meet father," I replied
sturdily. And forthwith got into my oilskin cape
and small sou'wester.

Poor mother made but feeble protest, for I was
big and determined of my age, and she must have
seen something in my mien that led her to hesitate
about telling me to stay at home. Moreover, she
probably longed secretly for my company and
support.

So leaving a bountiful repast artfully disposed
where it would keep warm without being spoiled,
we sallied forth into the tempestuous dawn, and
made our way toward the wharves, keeping the
lee of buildings, as seashore folk learn to do when
the winds are abroad, and waiting for a lull in the
tempest before venturing to scurry across the places
where it had full sweep.   All the fishermen's
quarter of the town was astir, and we gleaned here
and there bits of news from one neighbor and
another as we went.   All night the fishing fleet had
been coming in one by one, and a score of them
was safe at anchor by now.

"Was the 'Molly Pitcher' among them?"

Nobody knew.   Those whose menfolk were
known to be safe were so well content with their
good news that they had no thought as yet for the
grim uncertainties that still hung over the fate of
others.   So we pushed on and at length joined a
storm-lashed group that cowered behind the last
available shelter, whence we could look out across
the wind-swept harbor, and see great white rollers
bursting against the headland, and spreading themselves out in a vast sheet of whiteness along the
bar.

Quite a little swing of a sea made into the harbor
itself, and the sturdy fishing craft rode uneasily at

their hempen cables, even in those comparatively sheltered waters. The "Molly" was not among the anchored craft, as I knew at a glance, and so told my mother, who was not familiar as I with the individuals of the fleet. So we kept our eyes on the headland around which those that had weathered the gale off shore must presently begin to appear.

The light-keeper, meanwhile, on the headland across the harbor, well aware of the anxiety that must prevail at such a time, had set a signal on his flagstaff which said to the townfolk, " Nothing in distress is in sight." So all took heart of grace and hoped that the next vessel to come in would be their very own. We now learned for the first time that the minute guns heard in the night were from a large merchant-ship that had gone to pieces on Spanish Reef, and was apparently lost with all hands, for at daybreak no sign of her was visible from the shore, and the outer beach was already strewn with her wreckage. To do anything for her people, before the gale subsided, if any had managed to survive the night on the reef, was out of the question. Moreover, most of the able-bodied seafaring population had all they could do for the present to mind their own affairs. So we stood for an hour, women, and old men, and a few

children, keeping one another in countenance with
gossip and guesswork.

But, see! there is a dim something half obscured
with rain and spray driving in past the lighthouse.
It is a fisherman sure enough, and another is close
astern of her. On they come, under storm trisails
and with topmasts sent down, riding easily over the
tremendous seas that the ebb tide makes off the
headland. Evidently they are all right. But
what are their names? Old Captain Spencer, too
infirm to go to sea any longer, is on hand with his
spyglass at his eye, but he cannot yet make them
out. They come on, however, like racers, more
plainly in sight at every moment, and presently a
dozen voices, mine included, cry out joyfully, " It's
the ' Molly Pitcher,' " and my mother goes down on
her knees with her arms around me, and it is some
minutes before she can summon strength enough to
go home and make ready for her menfolk, who are
certain to be half famished after their all night
battle with the wild Atlantic.

I stayed behind to receive my father, nor had I
long to wait. For the " Molly " promptly doused
her storm trisail and made straight in for the shelter
of the breakwater under foresail alone. You may
be sure that I jumped the rail as soon as her fenders
touched the wharf, and was forthwith gathered up

in the arms of a great creature in shining oilers who dripped salt water where he stood and asked out of his wet beard if all was well at home.

Such are my earliest recollections of life. One may think that they should have filled my mind with horror and fear of this great insatiable monster, called the sea, who held up glittering prizes before the face of honest fisherfolk only to snatch them away, and leap hungrily at their throats when they trusted in its good faith. Yet, strange as it may seem, these happenings only made me long for manhood that I might take part in those wild encounters that seemed to me the only really worthy aim for a boy's ambition. Such and so strong is the instinctive love of physical excitement implanted in every spirited boy's heart, to the infinite perplexity of their mammas, who cannot comprehend why boys take naturally to guns, and boats, and games that are more or less fights, instead of to dolls and ribbons and gentler pastimes like the majority of their sisters.

But there came a time to me, as the like has come to many Stonyhaven boys, three years later, when the " Molly Pitcher " did not come sailing in with the rest of the fleet, and when some of the last of them staggered home over the bar under shortened sail, one set her colors at half mast as she dropped anchor, which signified either a death among her own crew or some other disaster involving loss of life. In this case it meant the worst possible for us. The "Molly" had foundered on George's Bank at the height of the gale, and all hands were undoubtedly lost. I was ten years old at the time and my mother, never very "rugged," as the New England saying is, left me alone in the world shortly afterward, having, however, set her modest house in order, and made me over to the care of old Dr. Shumway, as he was called by virtue of his office of principal of a select school for boys, which in its day was famous among its fellow institutions of learning.

The "doctor" was in fact a retired sea captain, who had commanded a troop-ship in the war with Mexico, and had his knee shattered by a musket ball in an encounter with one of the few Mexican cruisers that did any actual sea service during the year or two of hostilities. He had a battalion of regulars for passengers bound for Vera Cruz, and handled his ship so well, wounded as he was, while the soldiers were standing off the Mexicans, that the officers of the regiment united in a memorial to Congress that brought him an appointment in the navy and eventually gave him a comfortable pension, as was quite right and proper. After the

surgeons had done their best with his knee, however, he found himself no longer fit for sea service,
and, casting about for means of livelihood, bethought
him one day of school-teaching.

"I am not very much of a scholar," he said,
" but I know the three R's and English grammar,
and I am a first-rate disciplinarian; if any of my
pupils — that are to be — want any higher education than that, I'll find somebody that can teach
'em."

Now it happened that there stood on a rough
granite ledge, two miles or so from Stonyhaven
Port, an old gray gambril-roofed mansion, considerably antedating the Revolution in age, and enjoy-
ing an enviable local reputation as a haunted house.
For this latter reason it was for sale cheap, and
Captain Shumway was enabled to become its owner,
with the adjoining acres of poverty grass, and cedar
patches, and granite boulders, which were pictur-
esquely distributed over the hillside. A few hundred dollars judiciously expended repaired the
ravages of time and neglect, and the captain-
doctor, with his two maiden sisters, made short
work of the alleged ghosts.

The old house was renovated throughout; floors
leveled up where they had settled away from the
big central chimneys, timbers renewed where the

hard oak of a century before had crumbled to powder, sagging rafters replaced by new and straight ones, and the roof covered with thick split shingles from Maine (the captain would have none of the then comparatively new sawed variety), and the whole structure made fit for another century of usefulness. All this was effected without impairing the comfortable, dignified, colonial aspect of the exterior.

When the new shingles had assumed their weather stain of gray, the old house looked for all the world just as it did when the British were looting Stonyhaven in 1781 and storming the fort on the heights opposite. The captain and his sisters moved in with their old-fashioned furniture in late summer, and spent the ensuing winter in making things comfortable and getting to rights. Very comfortable and homelike they made the old mansion, and shortly after Christmas the captain issued a characteristic circular and prospectus, of which the following is a faithful copy : —

Captain Abner Shumway, late of the United States Navy (retired), will open a boarding and day school for boys at Rockledge, near Stonyhaven.

Reading, Writing, Arithmetic, and English grammar taught THOROUGHLY, if the pupil

*is capable of learning them.   If not he will be
taught something useful instead.*

*The so-called " Higher Branches" will be taught
if desired to the point of preparation for college,
but only after the pupil has actually learned the
essentials of a common education as specified.*

*Every boy will be taught to swim during his
first summer term.   Every boy will be required to
take a reasonable amount of exercise.   Every boy
will be helped to cultivate such artistic or mechanical gifts as Nature may have given him.*

Military or naval drills twice a week.

Modified naval discipline maintained at all times.

Then followed the rates of board and tuition and
the like, which were not so very moderate, but were
subject, as many a deserving applicant found, to
substantial reduction in special cases.   My own
was one in point.

I was, as I have said, left alone in the world
shortly after the great storm of 1854, which sent
the brave old " Molly Pitcher" to Davy Jones.
Dr. Shumway, as he was known in Stonyhaven,
or " captain," as he insisted upon being called when
on duty at Rockledge, was appointed my guardian
by my mother, and I can pay no higher tribute to
his memory than to say here that he did his duty

by me like an officer and a gentleman, managing
my little inheritance so judiciously that by the time
I came of age I had quite a comfortable investment
to my credit, although he had, as was quite right,
conscientiously charged up my educational ex-
penses.

By this time Rockledge was in the heyday of
prosperity. A queer, rambling, weather-beaten
structure it had become as its needs increased,
pretty well covering the crest of its granite ledge
that looked out to sea between the chops of the
harbor. It was built mainly of wood, though brick
and the underlying granite bore no inconspicuous
part in its construction. It had grown in a helter-
skelter sort of a way from the original structure to
its present dimensions with dormitories for fifty
boys and classrooms for as many more. The old
captain's circular hit the popular taste, and he was
overwhelmed with applications to receive pupils for
whom he had no room. Meanwhile he had been
his own architect and had conformed his plans for
additional room to the local irregularities of the
hilltop with a charming disregard of consequences.

Here the edifice was content with but one story;
there it temporarily climbed to three; and there
again, where it had been found necessary to span
a narrow gulley in the granite ledge, it was not

easy to determine where cellars or basements began
and stories ended. Withal, however, the effect
was quaintly picturesque, and in this present year
of grace artists and art students from the "summer
institute" down on the point and photographers
with all sorts of cameras walk indifferently past the
modern colonial and Elizabethan imitations with
which the vicinity has been decorated, and carry
away more or less unsatisfactory negatives and "im-
pressions" in water color of Shumway's old school.

It was to this quaint home that the captain took
me after the funeral was over, and for the first
week or so I was given a room away from the
other boys, where Miss Electa and Miss Becky,
the captain's sisters, could look after me till I
began to get over the mingled feelings of desola-
tion and homesickness that succeeded my mother's
death and the abandonment of my boyhood's
home. I cried myself to sleep the first two or
three nights, but then became accustomed to my
surroundings, which, indeed, were not altogether
strange to me, for my mother had taken me out
to the school on one or two occasions during my
younger days.

A short time after my arrival the captain called
me into his office — he never would allow it to be
called a study, because, as he said, he had enough

to do keeping school without studying — and told me as much as he thought necessary about my personal affairs and what he expected of me. Then he tried me on the multiplication table, which I did not know very well; made me read a few verses from the Bible and one or two sentences from the Constitution of the United States, and questioned me in each instance as to what I had been reading about. Then he asked me to spell a few commonplace words, and finally took me to the schoolroom, and showed me a desk pretty well up to the front. "You may sit here," he said, " and study, and look about you for two or three days, and listen to the recitations; perhaps you can decide for yourself which classes you ought to join."

From the schoolroom we went to the dormitory, and I was shown a tiny room under the roof just big enough for a narrow bed, a washstand, wardrobe, bureau and chairs, — all of the plainest and most substantial description, and all as neat as wax, thanks to the housekeeping care of Miss Becky, in whose department it was. This room, the captain told me, was my very own, and that I should be held responsible for it. Every boy, indeed, was required to sign a receipt for the room and its contents, just as an army or navy officer re-

ceipts for any government property when he takes
possession.

A brief set of printed rules of discipline and
behavior " in quarters " was posted on the wall.
Beyond these there were very few rules, indeed, but,
somehow, the entire school was permeated with a
boyish sense of honor that went far to counteract
the blackguardism that is apt to get the upper hand
where a lot of boys are thrown together and mis-
governed or not governed at all.

We were organized as a two-company battalion,
with full complement of captains, lieutenants, and
warrant officers, but official rank was recognized
only during official hours, that is, during school
and drill, and after " taps " at night, when everybody was supposed to go to sleep. Of course we
had our black sheep. Some of them capable of
reformation, others irreclaimable; but these last,
after having at least three chances to prove their
good intentions, had a way of quietly disappearing
over night, and it would be mysteriously whispered about the next day that they had been sent
home.

Whenever practicable, good government was
enforced by a sentence of a formally constituted
court-martial, the captain himself usually presid-
ing, and seeing to it that the laws of evidence

were duly observed, and all things done decently and in order. As I recall some of these trials, I think sometimes that the boys regarded the simple form of affirmation used with more reverence than is often accorded to the oath administered in so-called courts of justice. The captain would rise in his seat, and, calling the witness, make him stand in full view of all his schoolmates, facing them. "Now," he would say, "repeat after me, I, James Lynch," or whatever the boy's name might be, "promise on honor to tell the truth about the matters now to be brought before this court." And, as a general thing, the truth was told and a righteous decision reached.

But I fear I am making myself tiresome over this account of the manners and customs of the old school and the way it governed itself. We had, besides, plenty of boy fun, plenty of play hours, a good-sized and reasonably level playground back of the ledges, a swimming beach only a few hundred yards from the door, games of all sorts,— football that was real football, and did not make brutes of us besides; baseball that had not been reduced to an exact science; and a sturdy little schooner-rigged fishing smack, on which we cruised about the vicinity, under the proper supervision, in almost any weather, and which we learned to handle as smartly as any crew of man-of-warsmen could have done.

We had a loose-fitting uniform of blue jeans, with brass buttons, which could be worn either over our ordinary clothes or in warm weather by itself alone, and which answered very well for sea or shore duty, costing, if I remember rightly, something less than two dollars for the entire suit, including a sort of tam-o-shanter-shaped cap of white duck. Very smart the battalion looked, I can tell you, with its white belts and white canvas shoes, and we prided ourselves very greatly on our martial bearing and steadiness in ranks when we turned out for parade or marched into town on state occasions. Little did we guess in those days how many of us would in a few months be wearing other uniforms and finding the usefulness of our school drill on shore and at sea in more serious work.

CHAPTER II.

SECESSION AT ROCKLEDGE.

WE did not ordinarily pay much attention at Rockledge to political or national affairs, except that most of us were nominally either Whigs or Democrats, according to our bringing up. The young Republican party hardly guessed at its own strength then. There were in the school a number of Southerners, and five or six years after I became a pupil, when I had risen to be captain of one of the battalion companies, there began to be insensibly a certain drawing apart of these boyish representatives of the two great sections. Heretofore we had been friendly enough, barring the slight differences that result from home traditions, but Captain Shumway's training tended to make us all, as it were, a happy family together. The Kansas-Nebraska troubles began to mark the dividing line more clearly; then came John Brown's raid in Virginia (1859), and a certain intensifying of the anti-slavery sentiment in the Northern States. The election which resulted in the choice of Mr. Lincoln for president followed, and then Southern boys began to be called home by their parents.

After what I have said about my guardian it is hardly necessary to explain that he was eccentric, and with his eccentricities he possessed a certain faculty of prediction : I do not call it prophecy or foresight, for that rather savors of the supernatural, but he had that not uncommon gift among born disciplinarians of apparently seeing what mischief we boys were up to out of the back of his head, and if there was any scheme on foot for raiding a neighbor's orchard or melon patch he was pretty nearly certain to know about it beforehand and frustrate it in some highly original and effectual way that generally made us ashamed of ourselves. I cannot resist relating one instance of this kind. Billy Bunsby was, perhaps, one of the worst boys in school, the ringleader in most of the mischief that was perpetrated.

One day, while the crew of the gig was out, they discovered across the harbor from the school a promising melon patch, and Billy organized an expedition for the next night to test the quality of the crop ; the most profound secrecy was enjoined, and all the intending participants were pledged by solemn oaths known to boyhood. Nevertheless, when they started out, after having made their

escape from the dormitory undiscovered, they were
hailed by the captain just as they were shoving
off, and told that Deacon Giles had gathered his
entire crop of melons that afternoon. The boys
slunk back to their beds, of course, in the most
crestfallen mood, and somehow the whole story
leaked out the next day, and the participants in
the midnight raid did not hear the last of it for
many a day.

It will be readily understood from this that
among those of us who had any sense the captain's word was fairly good law in the school, and
his predictions regarding wind, weather, and
human affairs in general commanded profound
respect in his little kingdom.

The strict, local Puritanical observance of
Sunday made the day rather trying for half a
hundred boys, who had somehow to be kept in
order, and none realized this better than the captain. He used to give us all a tolerably long walk
to church, and when the weather was anyway
passible, would turn out the whole battalion just
after sundown, when, according to the New England creed, a little recreation, even on Sunday,
was admissable. After a short marching drill at
the double around the grounds up hill and down,
until all hands were pretty well blown, we were

fairly well disposed to keep still in the evening after tea.

It was his custom to give us informal talks on Sunday nights, especially in winter. It may seem incredible to men, who have once been boys and still remember it, when I say that these talks almost always commanded unflagging interest, even on the part of the dunces.

"Most as good as a circus," Billy Bunsby used to say reflectively, when one of them was over. Somehow, at this time of which I write all these talks had a more or less patriotic bearing, and I think, perhaps, that accounts for the fact that nearly every mother's son of us boys who was old enough served on one side or the other during the Civil War.

I remember with peculiar vividness, toward the end of 1860, after Mr. Lincoln had been chosen president, but before his inauguration, that, one evening, the captain rather overdid himself. At this period it was the policy of Southern leaders to misrepresent the character, wishes, and intentions of Northerners in every conceivable way. Perhaps they believed what they taught regarding Northern cowardice and general inferiority, moral, physical, and mental. At all events, they succeeded in leading their followers to death, de-

feat, and ruin, and to this very day they boast of
their achievement.

On this particular evening the captain looked
rather serious when the reading-hour came. I
cannot, of course, pretend to report what he said
word for word at this distance of time, but I think
I recall the gist of it. After rapping for silence,
he looked round for a moment, and then, turning,
unrolled a map of the United States and hung it
where we could all see it in the light of the hanging lamp.

"Boys," he began, "you don't any of you know
it, and I rather doubt if I can make most of you
understand, but you are all going to see some history made presently."

The phrase caught our attention. The idea of
turning out history ready made was certainly new
and fetching, and even the small boys who were
playing criss-cross on the sly in the corner stopped
and began to listen. I think they really believed
that he was going to take a lump of history out of
some one's hat, just as the magician had produced
a live pigeon at the performance we had witnessed
the week before. But the captain went on : —

"I don't bother you very much with politics, as
you know very well. I don't think many boys of
your age care much about it, but most of you have

heard more or less about Kansas and Nebraska and the John Brown raid, and, whichever party you or your families sympathize with, you must see that there is rather a disturbed state of things just now. That, in short, there is trouble brewing. I think I can feel it in the air, and you know by experience that I am something of a weather prophet.

"A lot of you boys are Southerners, and in your homes the servants are by law the property of your parents and guardians. All this seems perfectly natural and proper to you, and why should it be otherwise when you have been accustomed to it all your lives? And I can see that you may be very naturally indignant at any one who thinks that this is not the best possible condition of things.

"To us Northerners, however, it seems very unnatural. There are a great many things about it that we cannot understand, so you must make allowances for us — we must make allowances for each other. Most of us Northerners think that the South would be better off and more prosperous if the slaves could be set free, not all at once, but by slow degrees, so that they could have a chance to work for themselves. Some Southerners agree with us of the North in this respect. Here is a book very recently published of which something like two hundred thousand copies have sold already. I suppose that none of you have read it. I will merely say that it is written by a Southerner, that it sets forth the contrast between the commercial prosperity and general intelligence of the North and South, and ascribes to negro slavery all the blame for the existing state of things. Whether the author is right or not I do not pretend to say; but I know that the South is very much enraged at the publication of the book, and that it is almost unsafe for any bookseller to keep it in stock south of Mason and Dixon's line.*

" At any rate, the Southern leaders are afraid, now that a Republican president has been elected, that laws will be passed which may make slave property very insecure. I do not myself think there is any danger of this; I am an anti-slavery man, but I do not wish and I do not believe that one in a thousand of intelligent Northerners wishes to have slavery meddled with where it is. We merely do not want to have it extended, and we think with Mr. Helper, the author of this book, that the South

---

* The book referred to, entitled " The Impending Crisis of the South," was published in 1859, and in a few months went through many editions, and, strange as it may seem, probably bore a considerable part in exasperating the South against the North, which was precisely the reverse of the effect intended by its author, Mr. Hinton Rowan Helper.

will be very much better off if it will try to regulate slavery, rather than to extend it.

"I think, however, that the Southern States, or most of them, are going to withdraw from the Union. I think that most of you Southern boys will not be allowed to come back to school after the Christmas holidays. By that time your States will have passed resolutions withdrawing from the present Union. The government at Washington will have declared this action to be rebellion, and both sides will be getting ready to fight.

"Now, there are a number of you boys old enough and big enough for military service, either in the army or navy, and it is by no means impossible that some of you may find yourselves under arms before many months have gone. All of you have gotten some notions of discipline and drill into your heads since you have been here, and I hope you will do your duty wherever you are and, I will add, under whichever flag.

"Now I want to tell you what I think is going to happen, and you know I have had pretty good luck in hearing of secret expeditions before they come off" (a subdued titter ran round the room at this, for everybody remembered Billy Bunsby's recent experience). "Here is a map of the United States on which one of you fourth class youngsters may make a mark with this piece of charcoal separating the free and slave States."

After some hesitation, two small urchins stood up, and the younger of them was invited to step to the map and mark the division. I wonder how many schoolboys of his age can do it to-day?

But here came an unlooked-for interruption. Haines Gordon, a tall fellow from South Carolina, rose and "stood attention." We did not hold up our hands at Rockledge when we wanted anything, but simply stood up and kept still till we were noticed.

"Well, Gordon, what is it?"

Gordon swallowed hard once or twice; he was evidently under considerable excitement, but found his voice in a moment.

"Captain Shumway, the term slave State is very distasteful to us Southerners, and — and — well, sir, we don't like it."

The old captain's eyes flashed; it was a bold and unheard-of thing for one of his boys to do, arraigning him thus in the presence of the whole school. I could see that he was all ready to deliver a very cutting retort, if nothing more, but he checked himself.

"Very well, Gordon; I'll see what I can do."

He leaned his elbow on the table, and for a

moment shaded his eyes with his hand; then,
standing up : —

"Thank you, Gordon; it was inconsiderate on
my part, and I give you my word that it never
occurred to me before that the term might be offensive, but now I see it. To call any State a
'slave State' may certainly convey the idea that
the whole State is in slavery. While this is not at
all the idea that is intended, I will promise not to
offend again, but you need not expect the general
public to be equally considerate. The phrase has
found its way into the public prints, North as well
as South, and I am afraid it can't be got rid of.
But we won't use it here; we will call them the
'slave-holding States.' That is all right, isn't it?"

Gordon gave rather doubtful assent, but sat
down, having no reasonable objection to offer.

"Now, Martin," turning to the little map-marker,
who had been tiptoeing back and forth at his task,
"how do you get on?"

Martin had been standing at one side with the
pointer in his hand, and now traced the mark from
where the boundary between Pennsylvania and
Delaware touches the Atlantic Coast to the Ohio
River, then up and around Missouri, and across to
where California and Mexico lie side by side on
the Pacific.

"Very good, Martin; that will do. That is quite correct, as far as I see."

Martin received a little round of applause as he returned to his seat, for he was a well-liked little fellow among us.

"I am not at all sure," the captain went on, "that I can make you understand what a tremendous thing this is, and I do not think that I will even try. Martin's charcoal mark here stands for an actual line some three thousand miles long. It divides families, it cuts railroads and navigable water-ways; it separates planters and farmers from their markets, merchants from their customers, children from their parents. Now, as I said before, I believe that the slave-holding Southern States, or most of them, will assert their right to withdraw from the Union, and will attempt to do it. The Northern States will undertake to prevent this; the Union Navy will blockade the Southern ports, and after awhile Northern armies will invade the South. I say after awhile, for the South, by all accounts, is already well under arms, while here at the North we are going about our business very much as usual. We shall only wake up to our danger when we hear the Southern troops are marching on Washington.

"As a school, we have our work to do. I

know very well that there has already been some
skirmishing between North and South among you,
and I want to have you agree that it shall go no
farther. The Northerners far outnumber the
Southerners, and, moreover, we are at home
among our own people. In a sense, our Southern
schoolmates are our guests. Let us treat them as
such, and let me say to you Southern boys — I
think we are pretty good friends now, are we
not? — don't be too quick to take offence. We
have all got to stay here together, at least, until
your parents take you away, or you act so badly
on your own hook that I shall have to send you
home; let us be as happy a family as we can as
long as we can."

Upon the whole, the captain's address was well
received. Haines Gordon and most of the Southern boys came up and told the captain that they
would try and keep the peace. So did the leaders
of the New England faction. The older ones
among us were cool-headed enough to see that the
captain was right, and between us we managed to
keep the firebrands of both sections from being
fanned into a blaze. The Southern delegation
was practically eliminated after the Christmas
vacation, for South Carolina seceded in December,
several of the other States followed suit in Jan-

uary, and Virginia, last of all, in April. Southern families began to think it time to keep their boys at home, and when the summer term opened at Rockledge the music had already begun, but much had occurred in the meantime affecting my own personal fortunes.

CHAPTER III.

SHORTLY after the New Year of 1861, I being then just turned sixteen years of age, my guardian sent for me to his office. I was rather a good scholar for my years, and was pretty well along with the school course. Another year or so would have fitted me for the height of my ambition, namely, the examination for a cadetship in the naval academy at Annapolis, and until now my plans had all been shaped to this end. It had not occurred to me that any change was possible.

The captain, however, had been quietly turning things over in his mind, and on this particular evening he had something special to say. It was after nine o'clock. He never allowed himself to show me any favors because of the fact that I was a member of his family, and only on rare occasions was I summoned to a private interview.

"Jack," he began, without any preliminaries, "I am thinking of turning you adrift. You remember the tedious talk I gave the school when young

Gordon protested against my using the term 'slave States'?"

"Yes, sir; I should think I did remember it, though I don't recall its being tedious, as you say."

"Well, I don't want to brag, but I wasn't so very far out in my predictions, was I, now? South Carolina, Florida, Mississippi, Alabama, and Georgia have seceded and seized all the arsenals and ungarrisoned forts within their borders. Several weeks remain during which the old administration will be in power at Washington, and after the new one comes in it will be several weeks more before they can pull themselves together and decide what to do. Now, I remember well enough what I was at your age. What do you suppose I would have done if there had been a game like this called?"

"I'll tell you," I interrupted eagerly; "you'd have run away from home if your folks wouldn't let you go, and you would have shipped as a powder-boy in the navy or as a drummer in the army, wouldn't you?"

"Well, I rather think I should. And that is just what I don't want you to do, when we can work it quite as well otherwise. My old friend and shipmate Rogers is in command of the 'Constitution' at Annapolis; she is stationed there as a

practise-ship, you know; has a small crew of
'Jackies' on board to do the heavy work, and the
cadets go aboard now and then for gun drill and
the like. I've been corresponding with him, and
he says he'll take you as a sort of cabin boarder
for awhile; you can go on with your studies under
his tuition and get broken in to navy ways a bit.
Maybe something will turn up. Anyhow, think
of it over night and let me know how you feel in
the morning."

Think about it over night, indeed! As if any
doubt could be possible on such a question in the
mind of a Stonyhaven boy. Was I really to stand
on that quarter-deck, where Hull, and Bainbridge,
and Stewart had stood to see the British ensign
lowered on the " Java " and the " Guerriere," the
" Levant " and the " Cyane "? Was I really to
sling my hammock from the old oak timbers that
had shivered to the recoil of guns in action and
still bore scars made by cannon shot? There was a
singing in my ears at the thought, and every drop
of sailor-boy blood in my veins went coursing at
double quick.

"O Uncle Abner," I cried, forgetting in my
excitement that it was term-time, when I was not
allowed to address him by the title of adoption;
" do you really mean it? "

"Yes, my boy, I'm afraid I do. I'd like to keep you along with me and carry you a little farther in your studies, but the curtain is going to ring up presently on a drama, the like of which won't occur again within a century, and I want my Jack to see what he can of it."

So, after a little more talk, I went away in a high state of excitement to my little cot in the dormitory, intending to dream about sea-fights and all sorts of warlike experiences, including desperate encounters with fierce and piratical-looking rebels. But I thought instead — such is the unaccountable nature of dreams — that I was a good little girl at a Sunday-school picnic in pinafore and pantalettes, and with my hair done up in a long yellow braid. When I awoke and remembered what I had been dreaming about I was dreadfully ashamed of myself and thankful that the rest of the boys didn't know.

The next day was Sunday, and I am afraid I did not hear much of the sermon, for the plot rapidly thickened. Uncle Abner did not believe in an elaborate wardrobe for a sailor boy. Much to the horror of his soft-hearted sisters, I was packed off a few days afterward with nothing but a hand-bag; Uncle Abner going with me as far as New York, so as to see me safely aboard the train for Baltimore.

And so it came to pass that on a certain afternoon toward the end of January I found myself fairly south of Mason and Dixon's line in a sure-enough slave State, where the spirit of secession was boiling hot and all ready to burst the bonds of prudence. Several marines and sailor men were on board the Annapolis train, returning from shore leave, and to one of them I presently made bold to speak, showing him the letter that the captain had given me to present to Lieutenant Rogers.

He looked very knowingly at the superscription, as if he was constantly in the habit of reading handwriting, though I had my doubts, even at the time, whether he could decipher Uncle Abner's chirography.

"That's all right, sonny," he said. "I belong on the 'Constitution' myself; you'd best keep along with me when we get off the train, 'cause the rebs are getting mighty sarcy round Annapolis, and it don't do to go outside the academy grounds much alone."

So, bag in hand, I marched along beside my new acquaintance, who, with his hands in the pockets of his pea-jacket, rolled along, man-o'-war fashion, his wide blue trousers flapping about his ankles. He kept talking to me, in a voice that was music in my ears, albeit it was gruff with many years of

"WHERE ARE YOU GOING WITH THAT BAG, YOUNG FELLOW?"

sea service. He turned out afterwards to be a veteran gunner, who was a boy on board the "Essex" when Captain Porter fought a British squadron in Valparaiso Harbor, and while I remained attached to the "Constitution" our friendship was unbroken.

In the street of the town we passed a company of men in citizens' clothes, who were drilling with and without arms, and very black looks we received as we swung along toward the academy gates, taking no notice whatever of the uncomplimentary remarks that were now and then hurled after us.

We were not destined to go quite scot free, however, for the local secessionists had partly organized, and had already gone so far as to open recruiting offices in Annapolis and Baltimore. They even kept the government grounds under surveillance, and two men, with big revolvers in their belts and saddle-horses hitched near by, watched us keenly as we approached.

One of them stepped in front of us. "Where are you going with that bag, young fellow?"

"None of your business," said my escort roughly.

"Easy now, Jackey," said the man; "we've got orders not to let any strangers into the academy,

specially if they're carrying anything with them ; "
and he stepped forward as if to seize my bag.

" Orders be blowed," said my escort. " I've
got my orders, too. Come along, youngster."

But by this time the other man had me by the
collar, upon which my escort promptly knocked
him down, backed me up against the wall, and
squared off, as he said, " to repel boarders." Our
companions of the train, two or three marines, and
as many blue jackets had come along just in the
nick of time, and, though an ugly-tempered and
rough-looking crowd rapidly gathered about us,
the blue uniforms and stern faces representing
established authority had their effect; rebellion
was cowed, and we went on, passing presently
into the beautiful academy grounds.

My heart was beating high over this, my first
encounter with armed secession, and it was very
comforting to see the smart sentry, who, with polished equipments, walked his beat in front of the
guardhouse, and the formidable line of stacked
rifles, with a strong reserve of marines close at
hand ready to fall in at a moment's notice. Two
or three brass howitzers stood at commanding
angles among the buildings, and everything looked
ready for business, should occasion require. In
point of fact, however, the situation was very critical

within as well as without the government grounds. A large proportion of officers and cadets were more or less in sympathy with secession, and Captain Blake, the superintendent, hardly knew whom he could trust if Maryland should pass an ordinance of secession and attempt to seize government property, as some of her sister States had already done. His own son, indeed, an officer in the regular army, was an avowed secessionist.

My old gunner friend led me across the parade toward some lofty masts that towered over the intervening buildings, and presently we came out upon a kind of sea wall, whence I could see the gallant old frigate that was to be my home for awhile. She lay a short distance from shore, anchored bow and stern to keep her from swinging, and her grim row of thirty-two-pounders projecting through her port holes looked quite formidable to my unaccustomed eyes, although they were antiquated even in those days.

A clumsy, flat-bottomed ferry-boat took us alongside, and, my old gunner having privately instructed me how to salute the deck properly, we climbed the gangway, and I stood at last upon

" Her deck once red with heroes' blood
Where knelt the vanquished foe,

When winds were hurrying o'er the flood
And waves were white below."

The gunner and I touched our caps in due
form, reported "Come aboard, sir," to the officer
of the deck, and my new friend made known my
errand. Whereupon, a boy of about my own size,
and in a ship-shape sailor rig that aroused my
envy, was directed to take me to the captain's
cabin. We looked one another over somewhat
askance, as stranger boys always do, with a view
to possible future hostilities, and he led the way to
the break of the quarter-deck, past all sorts of
fascinating sea-going devices that delighted my
innermost heart, and finally knocked at a stout,
white door with a brass knob.

Ah, what a suite of rooms that was that I was
ushered into! Lighted by overhead skylights in
the quarter-deck, and by certain queerly shaped
stern gallery windows, it showed to the best advantage in the level rays of sun that streamed in
across the bright rugs that lay about the spacious
floor. The rooms were handsomely furnished,
but the objects that caught my attention were
several large, heavy cannon, covered with white
canvas, that ranged along the sides of the cabin,
and thrust their black muzzles outboard through

semi-circular cuts in the half ports. The commander's quarters were, in fact, really part of the main gun-deck, roofed in by the quarter-deck overhead, and forming part of the main battery when the ship was in action.

Lieutenant Rogers, in undress uniform, received me kindly, and his servant showed me a little cubby-hole below, where I was bidden to make myself at home. It was rather dimly lighted through a circular port, but had a bunk with some drawers underneath, and was very comfortable withal. Indeed, I was in such a state of mental exaltation that I should have been charmed with any quarters that had been given me on board the old ship.

It was not long before I had my modest belongings stowed away in what I was then pleased to consider man-of-war fashion. On returning to the cabin, Mr. Rogers questioned me a little about my studies, and then proposed that we should walk over to the superintendent's office and procure the necessary official authority for me to take up my residence on board. So he threw his loose, cape-like regulation coat over his shoulders, and I donned my own, which I gloried to find was not unlike the reefers worn by Uncle Sam's blue-jackets. Everything was new and fascinating;

the cadets in their tight-fitting uniforms on guard at the doors of the barracks, the exquisite neatness of the grounds, the long row of guns in the saluting battery, all appealed to the enthusiasms of my boyish nature.

The superintendent sat at his desk writing a despatch; behind him, stiff as a poker, was a marine, the orderly for the day, in full uniform. He stood in that graceful pose known as "the position of the soldier," his little fingers on the seams of his trousers, heels together, and feet accurately turned out at right angles.

"One moment, Rogers," said the superintendent, and, finishing the despatch, he handed it to the orderly, who saluted with his white-gloved hand, mechanically executed an "about face," stepped off, left foot foremost, and vanished. Hardly had the sound of his footfalls died away, however, when the superintendent, seeming suddenly to remember something, sprang up, and opened the window.

"Here, orderly," he called.

"Yes, sir," from below.

"Give my compliments to Mr. Marshall, and ask him to send two of the guard to the telegraph office with you with their side arms."

"Yes, sir."

" With side arms only, you understand."

" Yes, sir."

Closing the window and turning to Mr. Rogers, the old superintendent totally forgot my presence. " I wish I knew," he said, " where this thing is going to end. I have to send an escort for my orderly to go to the telegraph office. It's unsafe for a United States marine in uniform to walk through the streets of Annapolis. Here I've just got a cipher from the Department, telling me to exercise the greatest caution not to provoke hostilities. It doesn't say anything about resisting hostility, if they provoke it themselves. It's my notion that the honorable secretary just wants to nurse things along as they are till the fourth of March, and after that they won't care, for the other fellows will take their innings. By the way, how many men do you muster on board the ' Constitution ' now ? "

" Thirty-two, all told, sir."

" I must try and get you an additional draft. There's some secesh talk of getting possession of her."

Mr. Rogers flushed up to the roots of his hair. " You don't mean it, sir ! "

" Yes, but I do, though. Here's the very latest from Norfolk. Poor old McAuley is at his wits' end; he's got a lot of Southern officers at the yard, and they're badgering the old gentleman's life out of him. Oh, they won't try for 'Old Ironsides' yet awhile, but think what a feather it would be in the cap of the Confederacy if they could start their new navy with her for a flagship!"

"I'd like to see them try it, even with no more than my present crew on board; but I beg your pardon, sir; I came in to introduce Shumway's boy, the one that I spoke to you about a week or two ago. I'm afraid you've forgotten all about it, with all that you have on your mind."

The superintendent knit his brows and scowled at me in a way that rather made my heart quake. Mr. Rogers resumed: "Let me remind you; Shumway wants to get him into the navy in some shape in time to be of service to the country, and the boy himself is equally anxious to accomplish it. I find he's pretty well up in the essentials of navigation, and he is quite ready to ship as a powder-boy rather than lose the chance. He is to be my guest for awhile, and perhaps get ready for entrance into the academy this fall. His appointment is all arranged for, as I told you."

"Yes, I remember now," the superintendent said, glancing indifferently at me. "All right, make the most you can of him. We shall want all the good boys we can get, I'm thinking, before we're through with this business. Here, Moseley," this to his secretary, "make out a permanent pass for this youngster, will you, and bring it to me to sign." The formality was soon over, and I went back to my ship with a pass in my pocket authorizing me to come and go at will within the academy grounds.

Of my experiences during the next few weeks, I need not enlarge; I had my regular study hours, and spent most of my spare time on shore or in the rigging, watching the cadet battalion at its drills, gun exercise, fencing, and the like, until I had a pretty fair idea of what would be required of me if ever I joined its ranks.

On board the "Constitution" I occupied a rather peculiar position, being, as it were, one of the captain's family, and at the same time not prohibited by the strict considerations of naval etiquette from associating with the crew and with the boys of my own age, and learning all that I could about a seaman's life in the navy. My first acquaintance, the old gunner, retained a sort of fatherly interest in me, and put me up to a deal of naval lore, and tradition, and routine that I should otherwise have been long in finding out.

We had rather more than the usual complement

of boys on board, thirteen being the youngest age
at which boys were admitted to the navy; their
duties being to carry cartridges when the battery
was in action and practically do anything and
everything that was required of them, including a
somewhat uncertain period to be daily spent in
study under the supervision usually of some
warrant officer, who was supposed to be competent.

Two or three of these boys were decent fellows
enough, but the majority were a far rougher sort
than any that I had been accustomed to associate
with in my previous life. Several of them, however, I found quite companionable, and with one,
particularly, whom I will call Davy Jones,— the
same, by the way, who first led me to the captain's
cabin,— I became quite intimate. The most of
them looked upon me at first with some suspicion
as being a kind of a swell, whose intimacy with
the captain was not to be regarded altogether with
approval. The boys were regularly exercised at
gun drill with the lighter pieces, at single stick
exercise, which was the equivalent of cutlass drill,
and at any other of the lighter duties of a man-o'-
warsman.

Naturally, in view of the universal instincts of
mankind, the boxing and fencing were the favorite
exercises, and I soon learned that one of Lieuten-

ant Rogers' theories was that no considerable number of men and boys, such as make up the personnel of the navy, can live together for any considerable time without occasional and often salutary fights by way of settling disputes and establishing the individual relations that must always exist. The only rule — and that was an iron-clad rule — was "no fighting without gloves."

Many a quarrel which might have been serious was thus settled in a comparatively amicable way. Occasional knock-downs and broken heads naturally enough occurred as the result of quick and unforeseen quarrels, but there was a general understanding that in such cases the bystanders should at once interfere, send for gloves or the regulation single stick equipment, and make the contestants settle their quarrel according to rule.

Among the boys, of course, small fallings-out were more frequent than among the men, and I soon learned that I should have to find my level among my companions if life was to be anyway endurable. Accordingly, after thinking it over by myself, I decided to make a thorough job of it, and began by telling Davy Jones, with whom, as I have said, I was on most friendly terms, what I was going to do.

Davy grinned and wanted to know who I was
going to fight first.   I told him I thought I should
fight him.   We agreed accordingly to pretend that
we had had a quarrel, and fight to a finish that
same evening,—that is to say, until one or the
other of us was so pumped out that he could not
come to time.   When word was passed, therefore,
that there was a fight on at the fore section of the
main deck we had a very respectable audience,
and made believe glare at one another as though
nothing but life blood could satisfy our wrath.   In
fact, we were so nearly matched that, after a set-to
lasting some twenty minutes, we were separated by
the senior warrant officer present, who declared the
fight a draw.

There is a popular delusion to the effect that
black eyes and damaged noses cannot result from
encounters with soft boxing gloves, but our appearance, Davy's and mine, as we went to the water-
butt together, under proper escort to prevent us
from renewing the fight, would not have been
reassuring to our friends at home.

On reaching the captain's cabin, after having
performed a careful toilet, he saw in a moment
that I had been in a scrimmage, and, of course, I
made a clean breast of the whole affair, telling him
also that, if he didn't mind, I was going to fight

the entire contingent of boys, one after the other, beginning with the largest, just for practise.

"What a little gamecock it is!" he said, laughing heartily. "Well, I don't know that I mind, if you keep your tempers. You are all here to be turned into fighting material for your country's navy, and I don't know how you can get better practise."

Next day I went to look for Davy right after morning quarters, and found him forward with a good many of the men standing about. I went right up to him and shook hands, both of us grinning rather consciously over the fraud that we had practised, and each secretly aware that the fighting demon had been aroused in us toward the finish.

Jones had a very respectable black eye, and my nose was considerably enlarged from its ordinary proportion and not very pretty to look at.

Chance favored my plans so far as to cause the biggest of the boys to be standing close by, and I heard him say to a man next him : —

"Daisy nose Davy gave the old man's cub, didn't he?"

"What's that?" and I faced round toward him sharply.

"Oh, nothin', Jackey, my son. I was just admirin' of your cut-water."

" You called me the ' old man's cub.' "

" Well, what of it? "

" It's an insult, and I'm going to fight you. Will you fight? "

" Yes," he said, rather reluctantly.   " When? "

" As soon as my nose shrinks so I can see you," I said.

" Done," replied he.   ·

So the fight duly came off, and I was duly knocked out, as I expected to be, but I gave him more hard work than he looked for, and won no end of fame for my audacity.

After I had challenged and fought two or three more of the larger boys, I worked down into my own class, age, and weight, and very soon had no worlds left to conquer, for there was no boy of my size left on the list.   By this time I was easily the best boxer and swordsman on board, for the contests were occasionally varied by the substitution of single-sticks for gloves.   My reputation even spread among the cadets, and, as I was a member of Lieutenant Rogers' family, I began to be asked over to the fencing-room, where I speedily picked up bits of science that I should not have learned in the rougher tutelage of the main deck.

I am well aware that all this must seem very shocking to my gentle readers in this gentler age,

but, as Lieutenant Rogers said, "What are we
here for?"

With the aid of the older warrant officers, he
took good care that this kind of thing should not
go too far, and the result was that serious fights
were almost unknown among men and boys, and
we youngsters became a tough, active lot, with an
utter contempt for physical pain and a readiness to
endure fatigue and privation that served many of
us well in after days.

CHAPTER IV.

DURING all this time the storm clouds of
secession became more and more threatening along the Southern horizon. Early in February a provisional Confederate Congress had met
at Montgomery, Ala., and Jefferson Davis was
chosen president. The attempt to capture Maryland for the Confederacy had failed, thanks to the
loyalty of Governor Hicks, but his position was
very critical.

Baltimore, with its two hundred thousand inhabitants, was strongly in sympathy with the
South; the State capitol at Annapolis was equally
devoted to the same cause, and the national capitol
at Washington without adequate means of defense, with all the government departments at
least half filled with Southern sympathizers, and
it was even doubtful at the end of February
whether the president-elect could be brought safely
to Washington in time for lawful inauguration on
March 4. Reach Washington he did, however,

in spite of a well-organized plan for his assassination, passing through Baltimore in disguise a night or two before.

Then followed a painful period of suspense, while the rebels went on perfecting their civil and military organization and completing the investment of Fort Pickens at Pensacola and of Fort Sumter in the harbor of Charleston, the only two forts still held by United States troops. It was not until the end of March that the president and his advisers so far solved the legal and constitutional problems that confronted them that they could decide upon a definite course of action. It was then determined that the Rebellion had gone so far that active steps must be taken if the government would save itself.

All the available regular troops within reach had been summoned to Washington for the defense of the Capitol; but they numbered only a few hundred, and could not offer protracted resistance to the numerous battalions that were organizing across the Potomac. It was determined at last to send relief expeditions to the beleagured fortresses, and these were fitted out in New York with the utmost secrecy and despatch.

Everything was known, however, to the Confederate authorities, and on April 12 the bom-

bardment of Fort Sumter began. News of this
opening of hostilities reached Washington the next
day, Saturday, April 13, and on the Sunday following the president issued his proclamation calling out the militia of the loyal States to defend the
Capitol and aid in enforcing the laws of the United
States.

In those days the State militia, or, as it is now
called, the National Guard, was not so well organized as it is now; comparatively few regiments
were fully equipped with arms and field accouterments; fewer still were habitually drilled as battalions, and hardly a single company of volunteers
had at this time been organized. Nevertheless,
two days after the president's call was issued the
Massachusetts Sixth Regiment was on its way to
Washington, and on April 19, the anniversary
of the Battle of Lexington, it was fighting its way
through Baltimore, opposed by a furious mob of
Southern sympathizers.

Blood was shed and lives were lost on both sides,
but the regiment forced its way through to the
Washington station, and went on to the Capitol,
leaving the city and State behind it aroused to a
frenzy. For near a week it was a mere toss-up
whether Maryland should go over to the Confederacy or remain loyal to the Union. But the

governor, though almost overborne by the pressure
brought to bear upon him, steadily refused to call
an extra session of the legislature, and even delivered the State seal to General Butler, commanding
Massachusetts troops, for safe keeping, lest it
should be used in the official execution of some
compromising document. Meanwhile the Baltimore mob burned the railroad bridges, so that no
more troops from the North could go to the rescue.

At Annapolis we were for the time completely
isolated, getting our news only at second hand,
and poor Captain Blake, the superintendent of the
naval academy, was still further perplexed by the
arrival on leave of his secessionist son. The
old gentleman and his wife could not turn their
son out of doors, and were yet afraid to have him
within the lines. Still, he made the best of it, appealed to the young man's sense of honor, and,
so far as is known, his confidence was not abused,
and, although young Blake subsequently resigned
his commission and served in the Confederate
Army throughout the war, still he did not betray
his father's trust.

The chief anxiety of the little garrison at Annapolis was concerning the old "Constitution," though
little danger was to be apprehended from an attack
by land, for the academy grounds were surrounded

then, as now, by water on three sides and a stout
brick wall on the fourth. The approaches could
be easily commanded by artillery and riflemen,
but for the gallant old frigate there was no such
ready means of defense. To be sure, the senior
class of the academy was quartered on board
during part of the time, but no additional draft of
seamen from the navy could be obtained to fill out
her crew to its full complement.

Nevertheless, the best was done that could be
done, boys and all taking their turns at various
kinds of duty. Through my influence and intimacy with the commanding officer, I was able
sometimes to get myself and Davy detailed to con-
genial tasks, one of which was going aloft to the
main royal cross-trees with a good glass and keeping a lookout on the movements of Confederates,
in the neighborhood of the State capitol.

On the forenoon of one beautiful spring day
early in April, which in that latitude means green
grass and the trees pretty well leaved out, Davy
and I were perched in the cross-trees to relieve the
regular lookout for an hour. We were spying
about half carelessly, when one of us noticed some
movement in an old brickyard, where nothing had
been done for months, so far as we knew. We
could make out four negroes working about a

couple of old scows, apparently cleaning them out, but for what purpose, of course, we did not know.

After awhile, however, the scows were cast off from their moorings, and with two men in each working the big, clumsy sweeps, they passed out of sight into a little cove, which formed part of an estuary, known as Spa Creek, that makes up inland to the southward of Annapolis. We watched them out of sight without having our suspicion particularly aroused, and then chanced to see a couple of horsemen riding from the direction of the State capitol toward a point which would bring them not very far from where the scows had disappeared.

" Davy," said I, a sudden thought entering my head, " what bully good boats those would be to bring boarders alongside this old ship of ours."

Davy stared at me with mingled wonder and admiration.

" Well, I should say so," he said at last. " Maybe that's what they're up to. Let's go out sailing in the ' Junior,' and see where they've left those boats."

" Junior," short for " Constitution, Junior," was the name of a little sailing dingy in which we boys who knew how to manage a sailboat were allowed to cruise around in the vicinity of the sea wall and the academy anchorage. When we were relieved by the regular lookout, therefore, we slid down by the back stays, and got leave to go sailing.

Fortunately, we were favored by a clipping breeze, and a few minutes carried us out up the creek and past the mouth of the little cove which I have before mentioned. Just within the mouth of this an old canal-barge had grounded, and was now almost high and dry on the beach. Alongside of this our two brick scows had been moored end to end, and one or two men, with the negroes whom we had seen before, were standing about, apparently examining the situation.

We did not deviate from our course, lest we might arouse suspicion, as the "Junior" was known as part of the academy equipment. Having thus located our quarry, we headed back for the ship. and on the way concocted an elaborate scheme for the afternoon.

The usual hour of drill for the Confederate troops that were organizing in and about Annapolis was rather late in the day,— say, about five o'clock. We had often watched them marching and countermarching from some point of vantage aloft on the "Constitution," and we knew pretty well at what hour they would begin and when they would leave off. Putting these things together, we decided that if the brick scows meant any business at all one or more of the companies would be marched down there for practise that very afternoon.

The question was how could we both of us manage to get off so as to see them and learn what they were up to. Fortunately, the crabbing season was just beginning, and I knew that both Lieutenant Rogers and Captain Blake, the superintendent, were uncommonly fond of these delicacies. So Davy and I innocently asked leave to go crabbing that afternoon.

In the meantime all our leisure moments were devoted to busy preparation. We rummaged about among the cast-off sea toggery of the crew, and succeeded before long in fitting ourselves out with some half-worn overalls and shirts that had been cast aside, and finding some battered straw hats and blouses in rags, we rigged ourselves out as far as we could with our white faces so that we might pass for a couple of young darkies.

The perplexing question was "how should we blacken our faces." We had heard of using burnt cork, but, as we should have to change our complexions without the assistance of a looking-glass, we did not very well see how it could be accomplished in that way. Finally, I consulted

my old friend, the gunner, and he, being a person
of resource, like all good sailor men, forthwith
suggested lampblack and slush, ingredients of
which there is always a plentiful supply on board
a man-of-war.

At an early hour in the afternoon we had our
clothing and cosmetics done up in a portable
shape, had smeared over the sides of the "Junior"
with mud, which would be easily washed off, so as
to disguise her too familiar appearance, and leaving our sails behind, we pushed off and headed
across the creek so as not to give any indication
of our destination. I should have said that besides the ordinary equipment of crab fishermen we
had borrowed a three-inch augur from Chips, the
carpenter, and had also found some old wooden
bungs that would fit the hole it made. To each of
these bungs we had attached a piece of small line
some three or four feet long; besides this we were
ourselves provided with a coil of line something
like a hundred feet in length altogether.

Rowing along beyond the cove where the scows
were moored, we found the place beyond Windmill
Point where a grove of trees pretty well concealed
us from view, and there we proceeded to change
our clothes, and smear our faces, hands, arms,
and legs as far up as our knees with the not par-

ticularly agreeable mixture of slush and lampblack. One difficulty which had not occurred to
us now developed itself,— namely, our hair. That
it was not wool was perfectly obvious to the most
casual glance, but great are the powers of lampblack and slush, and we managed to trice our hair
up so that when concealed under our hat brims it
would pass very well for wool if the observer was
not too near.

By this time it was well after eight bells (four
o'clock), and all being ready, we pulled on into the
cove, and went to work catching crabs, imitating so
far as we could the lazy motions of the average
Annapolis darky.

There was no sign of life whatever about the
barge and its attendant scows, but we had fixed
half past five as probably the earliest hour for the
appearance of the enemy, so we possessed our
souls in patience. It was, in fact, between that
hour and six o'clock when we heard voices, and
presently the head of a column of infantry came
in sight out of a street which, if I remember
rightly, was named Charles Street, leading from
the direction of the State House.

These companies were not yet uniformed, but
they carried United States rifles, no doubt some of
those that were so generally distributed all over

the seceding States by the secretary of war, Mr. Floyd, and all their accouterments were in good shape. They swung along, carrying their pieces at the right shoulder, very good specimens of the splendid fighting material that formed the Confederate army. We counted the files as they turned along the beach before coming to a halt, and found that there were little short of two hundred men present.

They marched down the beach to a point opposite the old canal barge, and there halted and stacked arms. Of course, no two black boys out catching crabs for somebody else could be expected to go on with their work when a military company was drilling within sight. Accordingly, we stopped about two hundred yards off shore, and gazed with mouths and eyes wide open. Our appearance was so disreputable, I suppose, that it aroused no suspicions. At any rate, the drill went on, and we watched keenly everything that was done.

Evidently the officer in command understood his business. Probably he was a West Pointer or an ex-naval officer; at any rate, he instructed his men how to get on board the scows without massing too much on either side, and when they had learned that, he made them at a given signal

scramble up the side of the barge, which was considerably higher than the scows, and no doubt
represented in their minds the lofty sides of the
old " Constitution."

They were put through this drill several times,
with their arms at the last, until, with the ready
adaptability of Americans, they became proficient,
and the officer evidently thought that they would
be able to go through the same motion in the
darkness of night, and perhaps under the excitement of cracking rifles and bursting shells.

The sun was nearing the horizon and probably
most of the men were anxious to get home to their
suppers, being as yet volunteers not inured to
campaign habits in the matter of going without
their regular meals, so they were marched off just
before sunset, the officer making a little address to
them after they had fallen in behind the stacked
rifles.

We could not hear all that he said, but his voice
carried well in the still evening air, and we caught
a few words, the substance of which was, " Be
ready to turn' out under arms any time to-night."
Then followed the usual orders to march, and the
column passed off through the gathering dusk.

It may well seem incredible to any military man
of experience that such a drill could have been

performed and such instructions given almost
within sight of an enemy's headquarters, but it
must be remembered that these men were almost
in their own private dooryards; they knew that
they were surrounded by friends, and that any
spies or enemies could be watching them at that
time probably never occurred to the officer in
command.

There were, however, two very wide-awake
little darky boys, who a few weeks later would
probably have been referred to as contrabands,
watching all their movements with two very sharp
pairs of eyes and drawing their own conclusions
from what they saw.

We poled slowly along as soon as things had
become quiet, drawing in to the shore and gradually getting nearer to the scows as it became
darker. At length we slid in between the two,
fastened our skiff, and, taking our tools, scrambled
aboard the overhanging scow. The first thing to
be done was to look the boats over so as to be sure
of our ground; this took but a moment, as there
was sufficient light from the western sky to enable
us to see where we were going.

The scows, as we supposed, were simply flat
boats, clear of all thwarts and cross timbers amidships, and having merely a footboard crossing

them at either end. Measuring on the outside so as to locate the water line exactly, Davy started in at a suitable place to bore a hole through the side of the scow just where the water would not come in while the boat remained empty. Our respective duties had been arranged beforehand, and while Davy bored the hole I climbed over the side and made the end of a line fast to the side of the barge by means of a screw-eye that I had brought with me.

The bung, with its shorter line attached, was all ready, and while Davy finished the first augur hole, I promptly pushed the bung into it from the outside, and tapped it gently home. Then it was but the work of a second to tie the short line and the long line together, and we ran to the other end of the scow to repeat the operation. Two three-inch augur holes were made in each scow, and the lines secured and made fast to the bungs all inside of half an hour.

By that time it was pretty dark, and we hurried to gather up the fresh chips that had been made by the augurs, and get into our skiff as speedily as possible.

Now I think that the veriest landsman can understand that pushing off the scows would tighten the lines and pull out the bungs, and with a load of a hundred men the augur holes would be well under water, and it would take only a few minutes, with two three-inch streams flowing inboard, to send both boats to the bottom.

We had just finished boat number two when we heard voices and footsteps, which drew nearer, and Billy and I had only just time to scramble into our skiff and hide under the shadow of the overhanging bows when a corporal's guard of three or four men, with guns on their shoulders, came along the beach. Evidently the commander's mind had misgiven him regarding the safety of leaving his boats without protection, and he had sent these men to be at hand until the time for action came.

"Stay here, boys, while I go up and see that everything is right," said the man in charge.

We lay low as possible in our little skiff, and heard the corporal walk up the gang plank and march back and forth slowly the whole length of the barge. Apparently his inspection of the scows was satisfactory, for we heard him go back and descend the gang plank, rejoining his companions on the beach. A short colloquy ensued as to whether the party should make its temporary bivouac on shore or on the old canal barge, but it was finally decided in favor of the former, and we presently heard the men gathering wood for a fire and making themselves comfortable.

This was the signal for us to shove off and make our way home before the light of the fire would endanger our safe retreat.

It was nearly eight o'clock when, half famished, wet, and tired, we reached our ship, after a most exciting afternoon. Climbing the gangway, we got on deck, and found some difficulty in getting ourselves recognized by the quartermaster on duty, who held up his lantern and scrutinized our black faces with suspicion and amusement.

After we had convinced him who we were, he said that Mr. Rogers had left orders that on our arrival we were to report immediately to him. Accordingly, without stopping to put ourselves to rights, we went to his cabin, and, in answer to his summons, advanced within the circle of light. Knowing nothing of our designs beyond the mere announcement of a crabbing expedition, he had no reason to anticipate anything beyond the ordinary smartly dressed sailor boys whom he was in the habit of seeing about his ship.

When his eyes fell upon us, black, tattered, wet, and generally disgraceful, an expression of utter amazement spread over his countenance. Looking keenly at us for a moment, he seemed to recognize us. We pulled our forelocks and reported as usual. After trying for a moment to

retain upon his features a stern expression of
severity, he gave it up and burst into laughter.

"Well," he said at length, "what mischief
have you two been up to?"

Billy and I glanced rather guiltily at one another, and I suppose his eyes told me that he
thought I had better make a clean breast of it. So
I told him in a few words how our suspicions had
been aroused, what we had discovered in the forenoon, and what steps we had taken after our suspicions were confirmed to disable the equipment of
the expedition.

"Why didn't you report to me what you saw in
the morning? That's what you ought to have
done."

"Well, you see, sir, there wasn't anything to
report. Just those two brick scows, and we
thought if we said anything about it we should
simply get laughed at."

After a little cross-examination, Mr. Rogers rose
suddenly and dismissed us, saying, "Get yourselves cleaned up, and come right over to the
superintendent's office."

We ventured to disobey orders in so far as to visit
the cook's galley on the way, where we managed
to beg a bit of hard tack and a cup of coffee, before going on an errand which might detain us for

some time. Changing our clothes was a simple matter, but the slush and lampblack refused to yield kindly even to soap and hot water. After spending all the time we dared in vigorous scrubbing, we started for headquarters.

The orderly on duty grinned when he saw our still smutty faces, but ushered us immediately into the presence of the grim old superintendent, who was sitting in his office with Mr. Rogers, evidently in consultation.

We stood side by side, caps in hand, toeing an imaginary seam in the deck, and awaited developments. Captain Blake looked us over very keenly, glancing sternly from one to the other for a moment, and then, seeing that neither of us winced, he relaxed his official manner a little.

" Mr. Rogers tells me," he said, " that you boys think you have discovered a rebel plot. Tell me what you have seen." Then, as we both hesitated to begin, he added, " Which of you is the elder? "

" I am the oldest," said Davy, " but he planned it all out, sir ; " and he pointed at me with his left thumb.

" Well, go on."

So Davy gave a tolerably coherent account of how our suspicions were aroused, and how we

were afraid we should not be allowed to go at all
if we told what our real purpose was, and how we
effected a change of clothes and blackened our
faces over beyond Windmill Point. He went on
with his narrative without interruption until he
came to the augur, then Captain Blake interrupted
him.

"Augur," said he, "how came you to have an
augur?"

"We borrowed it of 'Chips,' sir — the carpenter,
I mean, sir — and we rigged the lines to the bungs
before we started out, sir."

"Bungs," asked the captain.

"Yes, sir, to plug the holes with, sir." Davy
glanced apprehensively at me, for he was beginning
to get rattled under this fire of cross-examination.

"Well, and what next?" said the captain, now
trying hard to keep from laughing.

Davy was speechless, so I had to take my turn,
and, being more accustomed than Davy was to
public speaking, I succeeded in making all the
doubtful points clear to the officer's mind.

Before I had finished they both appeared to be
in very good humor, and I even detected them
winking at one another when they thought we
were not looking.

"Rogers," said the captain at last, " I do believe

these young rascals have unearthed something of importance. Here, Benson," said he, turning to me, " show me just where the barge and boats lie, on this chart."

He laid the harbor chart on the table, and I was able to locate the position of the barge with almost perfect accuracy, because a small wharf was indicated on the chart quite near the position of the barge.

" Now, boys," said Captain Blake, " you may go and get a good supper. I shall want one of you to go out on the patrol boat later. Rogers, stay here a few moments I want to see you." So we took our departure, each of us wild to go on the expedition.

While swallowing the supper that the good-natured cook had kept for us, we drew lots as to which should volunteer, but the loser always refused to abide by the result, and at length we patched up the excuse that we must both go anyhow, so Davy conveniently forgot certain things, and I forgot certain others, and when we were examined as to our qualifications it became perfectly evident that only by taking the two of us along could the patrol boat expect to reach its destination safely.

During all these nights of anxiety a regular

patrol boat went on duty at sundown and cruised about all night in the vicinity of the academy water front. The usual beat of this boat was, of course, well known to the rebels, and it was arranged that an extra boat should be sent out a little before midnight, as it was morally certain that no movement would be made on the part of the enemy until after that hour.

A cutter was made ready, and a crew of a dozen picked men selected to go out in charge of Mr. Findley, a young officer of some experience in actual service. All were well armed, except us two boys, who, to our unspeakable disgust, were considered too young to be entrusted with firearms under excitement. However, we were well enough content to be allowed to go at all, and we succeeded in getting a little sleep before we were called to turn out at midnight.

That was the first boat expedition that either of us ever took part in, and I suppose we shall never forget the silent embarkation, the carefully muffled oars, and all the precautions usual on an occasion requiring perfect secrecy. We pulled directly across the creek to Sycamore Point, and then skirted the shore till we could cross over without the least risk of being observed.

Carefully keeping behind the rude wharf that I

have mentioned, which was between the barge and the creek, we took shelter among its upright piles where we were well concealed in the dark shadow. The bivouac fire still smoldered on the beach, and we could dimly make out the forms of three men sitting about it, while a fourth marched up and down to keep himself awake and on the alert.

Detailing two of our own men to watch, the rest of us made ourselves as comfortable as we could on the thwarts and on the bottom of the boat, and awaited developments. It was a long watch, and, in spite of the extra jackets we had brought with us, we found a chill striking to our bones. Most of us, however, went to sleep after awhile, but at four bells (two o'clock, A. M.), some one shook me gently out of a sound sleep, and I found that everybody else, including Davy, was wide awake.

"They're coming," whispered Mr. Findley. "Quiet, men," he added; "for heaven's sake, don't make a sound." This in the lowest possible tone that could be heard by the men in the boat.

So still was it, however, that we could hear every movement of the approaching party. They came along without any special precautions, carrying three or four lanterns, and scarcely

lowering their voices. Only about half had their
rifles with them. But all were provided with
heavy revolvers, as we could see by an occasional
gleam of reflected rays from the lanterns.

The commanding officer halted them on the
beach and reminded them of the afternoon's drill,
cautioning them against haste and confusion that
might be the natural result of unaccustomed conditions in the darkness. Then, taking his stand
by the gang plank and stationing men with lanterns where they would be most useful, he started
the embarkation.

We could see the long succession of dark figures
in silhouette against the dim lanterns, passing one
after the other up the steep gang plank. It took
nearly half an hour to get them all on board and
safely bestowed, seated, each in his own place, on
the bottom of the boat. The officer in charge, with
his lieutenants, superintended every part of the
embarkation, and at length remained standing
alone on the barge.

"All right on board No. 1?"

"Yes, sir," came the answer.

"No. 2 all right?"

"Yes, sir."

"Then cast off the mooring lines and prepare to
shove off."

At this he swung himself down into one of the
scows, and we could hear the oars run out and
the gurgling of the water, as the heavily laden
boats were pushed sidewise away from the barge.

In a moment they floated clear and we could
hear the men getting out their sweeps and beginning to paddle slowly ahead. Now came the
critical time. Only Davy and I in that cutter knew
exactly how the work had been done that was
intended to disable the expedition. You can
imagine that our hearts beat high with excitement,
and indeed everybody on the cutter was nearly
as excited as we, though their maturer years enabled them, perhaps, to hold themselves in a little
better. Everything seemed progressing satisfactorily; the loaded boats had drawn clear of the
barge, when swish, snap, as of something cutting
sharply through the water and bringing up with a
jerk.

" What was that? " asked a voice.

" Avast pulling."

More swishing and snapping as the different
lines tightened.

Evidently some of the oarsmen knew what
" avast " meant and others evidently didn't.

" Stop rowing, you lubbers ! " the officer roared,
seeing that the order was not understood.

There was a moment's silence and a whispered consultation. Then a voice with the characteristic drawl of the eastern shore spoke out: —

" Say, cap, I am a-settin' in about five inches o' water."

" So be I, and I," came from various parts of the two boats.

In our own cutter at this stage of the proceedings was developed an almost irrepressible desire on the part of the men to laugh and cheer. It was perfectly evident that our plan had succeeded, but a word of warning from Findley enabled us to keep ourselves under control, and at the same time the word was given to pass the cutter astern out from under the sheltering wharf. The men reached over, shoving against the piles with their hands, and sent the boat out under the still starlight. Concealed by the intervening wharf, we got our oars, and a few strokes sent us within hailing distance of the enemy, who apparently had not discovered our presence.

The subdued talk among them had now given way to a babel of noises, as the scows settled down, and hurried orders were given to search for the leaks and light the lanterns which had been extinguished. It was impossible to do anything in the dark. The water, however, was but shallow, and there was little or no panic among the sinking crews. Most of them could swim, and those who could not stood on the partly submerged scows, and easily kept their heads above water.

We could only guess what was going on rather than see, for the darkness was very dense. From snatches of sentences we knew that the fight was pretty well taken out of our Confederate friends. At last Findley stood up and hailed.

" Hallo, there ! "

No answer, but an ominous silence. The talking and splashing ceased.

" Hallo, there, I say ; who are you ? "

Still silence.

" This is the United States naval patrol boat. Answer, or I'll fire."

Here some crazy desperado, who had managed to keep his revolver dry, fired at us, the bullet singing past just over our heads and cutting the water beyond.

" Steady, there," shouted Findley sternly, for he heard a number of ominous clicks as our own men cocked their big navy revolvers. " Don't fire without order."

Then addressing the half-drowned secessionists, " I don't know who you are, but don't try that again. I could kill you all where you stand if I chose to give the word. If any of you are in danger of drowning I'll set you ashore. You don't want any help? No? Well, good-night, then. Oars! Give way all," and setting the helm hard aport, the smart cutter swept past the forlorn and baffled Marylanders, who, as we afterwards learned, all got safely ashore. Our crew pulled home in high glee, and Davy and I came in for much slapping on the back and rough congratulation.

Next day the local secessionist paper contained the following paragraph :—

"Two companies of the 1st Maryland infantry, under command of Major MacKenway, started out last night on what promised to be a successful expedition, aimed to secure certain property of the United States which may prove useful for the use of the Confederacy. The expedition was to go by water, and was safely embarked shortly after midnight. After leaving the wharf, however, the boats were found to be leaking so badly that it was necessary to abandon the expedition and return to the shore. Major MacKenway and his men were greatly disappointed at having to give up what seemed an excellent opportunity to try their new weapons on the tyrant invaders. But their time will come! Maryland will not long endure the sight of Northern mercenaries on her sacred soil! But for the weakness of certain State officials we should long since have been rid of this incubus."

CHAPTER V.

BY this time, having learned the routine of a boy's life in Uncle Sam's service, I was anxious to enlist and become a regular man-o'-warsman so far as a boy of my age could accomplish this end. But Mr. Rogers dissuaded me.

"Wait awhile," he said. "If this thing tides over, and we do not come to blows with the seceding States, you can enter the academy as a naval cadet without any interruption. Whereas, if you enlist now, you'll find yourself tied up and unable to make a choice of stations. But, if worst comes to worst, as now threatens, we can get you drafted into a good ship that is likely to see service, and you will learn more in six months than you would in two years of academy life."

I am afraid that in those days we youngsters longed for nothing so much as for war. The little taste of adventure that we had, simply stimulated the desire for more, and we could not be expected to foresee or appreciate all the horrors that actual war implies. To us it meant no end of excitement, possible promotion, and prize money, and, in short, all the fascinating phases of life that ordinary boys only find in the pages of novels. In short, we were full of fight, and the uniformly surly conduct of the few Confederates that we had thus far encountered only served to make us the more eager.

Shortly after this time came the attack on Sumter, news of which reached us a day after it had taken place. Then followed rumors that the president had issued a call for troops, that regiments from the north and east were making their way to Washington, and that there had been actual fighting in Baltimore.

Of the details we knew nothing; but the air was full of rumors, and if half the stories had been true of the concentration of Maryland troops in the vicinity of the State capitol it would have taken a very large Yankee army to resist their onslaught. We noticed, however, that there was less drilling of new levies in the streets after it became actually certain that Massachusetts troops had marched through Baltimore.

The railroad leading from Annapolis toward Washington was torn up, nearly all the rolling stock having previously been taken away. We were almost wholly without trustworthy news. Of course the vigilance of the sentries was redoubled, and a sharp lookout kept at night, the chief danger being anticipated from the water side, since it was thought that a hostile expedition could be readily sent down the Chesapeake from Baltimore.

Accordingly, when there was a sudden call to arms at about three o'clock on the morning of April 20, it took only a few minutes for all hands to be at their stations. The patrol boat, it seems, had showed its danger signal, and the different sentries and lookouts had passed the word along. Drums were soon beating the long roll, and everything was in readiness to repel an attack in short order. Presently we could make out the dim outline of a steamer coming up the harbor, but whether she was friend or foe we had no means of ascertaining, and orders were given not to fire until more accurate knowledge could be obtained.

She came to anchor in absolute silence, and in a few minutes a boat put off toward her from the superintendent's landing. Then came another long wait, and then the report that the steamer was the ferryboat " Maryland," from Havre de Grace, which had been seized by Massachusetts troops

under General Butler and pressed into the service
as a transport.

Captain Blake, who was himself a Massachusetts
man, went on board as soon as he received the
welcome intelligence, and an eye-witness of the
meeting says that the old gentleman broke down
and cried like a child when he shook hands with
General Butler, and the first words that he managed
to enunciate were : —

" General, will you save the ' Constitution?' "

General Butler at first, according to his own
account, thought the captain was taking leave of
his senses, and was referring to the Constitution of
the United States ; but he quickly reassured him,
and the old sailor's anxiety was relieved when he
looked around upon the thousand well-armed
though somewhat untrained Bay State men, who
had thus unexpectedly arrived to his rescue.

The presence of the Massachusetts troops
aroused grave apprehensions in the minds of the
local authorities. The governor, although loyal at
heart, was oppressed by an ever-present fear lest
some hasty act should bring on actual hostilities,
and he immediately protested officially and otherwise against the landing of troops on the sacred soil
of Maryland. General Butler, however, was not
very much given to standing on ceremony, so the

troops were landed in short order and in spite of
protests. Friendly relations were before long
established, and the once haughty and belligerent
mayor of Annapolis applied within thirty days for
the position of post sutler.

Before the general landing was effected two
companies were detailed, at Captain Blake's request,
to go at once on board the " Constitution " and
help her short-handed crew, acting at the same
time as a marine guard. These two companies
came respectively from Salem and Marblehead,
and a large portion of their numbers were sailor
men. Fore-and-aft sailors, it is true, but having
the adaptability of Yankees, and quite ready to
learn the ropes on board an old-fashioned square-
rigged frigate.

It was very amusing to see them fraternize with
the regular blue-jackets, and still funnier to see
Lieutenant Rogers adapt his old-school ideas of
naval discipline to the circumstances. He knew
very well that free and easy Yankee fishermen of
northern New England could not come down to
quarter-deck etiquette all of a sudden, so he governed himself accordingly and got as much work
out of them as another man would have gotten out
of double their number.

The ship had to be lightened of her guns before

she would float, and her huge anchors had lain in one place so long that they had settled down many feet into the mud. But many willing hands made quick work. The "Maryland" was brought alongside, and the big guns hoisted on board of her in short order. Then the old-fashioned capstans were manned, and by main strength the anchors were hove up out of their deep bed. Everything was clear at last and the "Maryland" towed us out into the deep water of Annapolis Roads.

That night the "Constitution" once more rode freely to her anchors, and if ships are sentient beings, as some sailor men hold, her old timbers may have thrilled with memories of the past. Never before had she more narrowly escaped having her honored flag lowered and an alien emblem hoisted in its place. But now she was afloat once more, and, singularly enough, manned and guarded by descendants of the very men who built her in 1797 and fought her so gallantly in 1812.

Next day the New York Seventh Regiment arrived by steamer from Philadelphia, and after a short delay both regiments started for Washington overland, reaching the Capitol without opposition and in time to reenforce the slender garrison of regulars and hastily gathered volunteers that had thus far been the only guarantee of safety.

It is one of the strangest facts in connection with this period of the Civil War that, with all their ability and all the means at their disposal, the Confederate leaders did not seize the Capitol at Washington when it was in a defenseless condition. That they could have done this almost without opposition is now generally conceded, and if they had done so they would probably have had little difficulty in securing the recognition of foreign governments and in practically placing the Northern States on the defensive. The border States, as they were called, would no doubt have quickly joined the Confederacy, and the history of the North American continent would have read very differently.

After the departure of the troops, Annapolis was left in comparative quiet. But it was presently decided by the authorities to move the whole academy establishment to Newport, R. I., until hostilities were over. Annapolis was too near the border land of actual hostilities, so, after as little delay as possible, all hands were embarked on board the " Constitution," and after an uneventful voyage of three or four days she dropped anchor in the harbor of Newport.

This trip gave me my first taste of actual sea life and ended my relations with the fine old frigate. From Newport I ran over to Stonyhaven and renewed my acquaintance with schoolmates and scenes that I had left two short but eventful months before.

CHAPTER VI.

MUTINY OR TREASON?

WITHIN a few days after the opening of hostilities in Charleston Harbor, the president issued a proclamation announcing a blockade of the entire coast of the United States south of the Chesapeake,— a measure which excited boundless ridicule in the Confederacy, and was sneered at by enemies of the United States all over the world.

According to the law of nations, a blockade must be effectual in order to be binding. That is to say, all the accessible harbors must be guarded so that merchant vessels can neither go in nor come out. A simple notification to the world that a blockade has been established is not sufficient. When, therefore, the president of the United States, who had only about two dozen effective war steamers at his disposal, announced a blockade of three thousand miles of seacoast, everybody laughed and said it was a paper blockade.

But now that the aggressive policy had actually

been adopted by the new government at Washington there was no lack of energy on the part of army or navy. Vessels that were ready for service were promptly despatched to stations off the more important ports. All sort of craft, from ferry-boats up to ocean steamers, were purchased, volunteers were enlisted, vessels were armed as rapidly as possible, and in a surprisingly short space of time even the English and the Confederates themselves were forced to admit that a reasonably strict blockade of the Southern ports had been established.

The world's supply of cotton came at that time from the Southern States. English mill owners bought up every pound of cotton that they could lay hands upon, and the price naturally went up with a jump in all the markets of the world.

Then it was that the possibilities of blockade running dawned upon the British mind, and ship-builders were presently busy fitting out swift steamers of light draft and low free-board that could slip into any of the hundred rivers and harbors between the Chesapeake and Cape Canaveral. Painted lead color, such vessels are invisible on a moderately dark night at a hundred yards distance, and the chances were largely in their favor if under the management of daring skippers and skilful pilots.

The world wanted the Confederacy's cotton, and the Confederacy wanted the world's war material and general merchandise. The magnitude of the trade that immediately sprang up surpassed belief. The three most available American ports on the coast were Wilmington, Charleston, and Savannah, and within a short run of them were the British islands of Bermuda and Nassau.

Never before have these two crown colonies of Great Britain enjoyed such a period of prosperity as during those four years of Civil War. They were awakened suddenly from their long period of quiet, and, after a brief career of bustle and money making, they dropped again into their natural state of quiescence, from which it is not very likely they will ever be aroused.

Before the day of these professional blockade-running steamers, and, indeed, throughout the war, small sailing vessels played their part along the coast; beginning on the Chesapeake, they drove a brisk trade for a short time, but a fleet soon gathered in Hampton Roads that made escape to sea well-nigh impossible, and the Potomac flotilla soon cleared the shores of batteries and put a stop to local defiance of Federal authority.

Shortly after the proclamation of the blockade the opportunity came for which my sponsors, unbeknown to me, had long been watching. The old sailing sloop-of-war, "Wakulla," which had been on the China station on a three years' cruise, came home unexpectedly. She was homeward bound in the regular order of things when the secession fever broke out. Orders countermanding her return were sent to intercept her at the Cape of Good Hope, as they were also sent in the case of many another United States cruiser that was, conveniently for the Confederacy, absent at some distant foreign station.

Luckily, the "Wakulla" was driven far to the southward out of her course; so far, indeed, that it was not worth while for her to work back to Cape Town. Therefore, she most fortunately missed the order sending her back into the Indian Ocean, and instead shaped her course direct for Newport.

She had left Hong Kong early in January. News did not travel around the world so rapidly in those days as it does now, and the result of the presidential election at home had not reached the China station. During her long voyage she had not fallen in with a single vessel that could give her news of the situation, and when she cast anchor off Fort Adams her people were entirely ignorant of all that had taken place.

Lieutenant Rogers recognized her as she came up the harbor, and ordered out his launch to go on board shortly after she had cast anchor, taking me with him. They had picked up a pilot off shore, and from him had got some inkling of the over-turning that had taken place since they had any news. Naturally, however, he had been busy with his duty of working the ship into harbor, and the whole company was in a state of suppressed anxiety and excitement.

Recognizing the old "Constitution" and our boat as a probable source of trustworthy informa-tion, all the officers crowded around the gangway as we came on board, and Lieutenant Rogers was almost carried aft to the quarter-deck, whither I followed him, almost unnoticed amid the excite-ment.

Few men could have been better qualified than he to answer their questions and tell the story of secession, as well as he could for the constant interruptions, so far as it had gone. I had mounted unnoticed upon the quarter-rail, whence I could both see and hear; and, boy as I was, I was pres-ently aware that there was a division of sentiment among the "Wakulla's" officers.

The captain, a South Carolinian by birth, as I afterwards learned, did not hesitate to show his pride and gratification at the action of his State and the result of the bombardment of Sumter. Several of his subordinates, while less outspoken, were evidently in sympathy with him. But I was glad to see that a majority of the officers were apparently deeply shocked, not only at the occurrences that had taken place, but at the apparent lack of loyalty in their brother officers. To all this I was listening with absorbed attention when I felt some one pluck my sleeve from behind. Looking down, outside the rail, I saw a weather-beaten blue-jacket standing in the chains and looking up anxiously at me. He could not be seen by the officers on deck.

"Say, youngster," he whispered hoarsely, "come forard, won't yer? Come forard and tell us Jackies about it; we don't know nothin'."

"All right," I replied, and slipped quietly to the deck. My blue-jacket friend joined me in the waist, and I was soon the center of a dense crowd in the wake of the forecastle, whose mutterings and black looks more than half frightened me as I found myself in the midst of them.

They had evidently picked up enough of the news to be in a state of intense exasperation. My head came barely above the average of their shoulders, and the fire of savage questions, uttered in a sort

George Gibbs 95

OLD ABE WAS ELECTED, HE SAY

of suppressed tone so that the voices should not be
unduly raised, almost took my breath away. I
answered, however, as best I could, till the eager-
ness of those on the outside of the circle burst the
bonds of naval etiquette.

"Louder, young 'un; we can't hear yer," and
the like; till at length some one sung out, "Set him
up on the capstan."

This last cry was taken up and became so general and imperative that I was summarily seized
by legs and shoulders, and quickly but firmly
placed upon the broad, circular top of the capstan.
Around me thronged the blue-shirted crew, who,
reenforced by those who happened to be below
decks, now nearly covered the topgallant forecastle and perched upon every available point of
the near rigging.

"Now, young fellow, give it to us straight.
'Old Abe' was elected, you say. Go on, what
next?"

"Well, then South Carolina seceded."

"What's that? See what?"

"Seceded, you lubber; cut adrift from Uncle
Sam, that's what." This from one of the men
who stood near the capstan.

"Go on, youngster."

"Yes," I continued, "South Carolina seceded,

and then the rest of the slave States seceded, too,
— most of them, that is."

" How about little Delaware?"

" She's all right!   Didn't secede."

" Ror for the ' blue hen's chickens ! " *

A dozen voices questioned me about Kentucky
and Tennessee; but these States were still in
doubt, and I could not say whether they were
saved to the Union. As well as I could for constant interruptions, I told them about the fall of
Fort Sumter and the burning of the Norfolk navy
yard, and I couldn't resist the temptation of telling
the part I had borne in saving "Old Ironsides"
from capture in the harbor of Annapolis. I need
not say that this elicited sundry cries of " Bully
for you, youngster," and poundings on the back
that made me see stars.

Then at last I told them that the blockade had
been ordered, and that the Northern States were
rallying to the defense of the Capitol at Washington. I never expect to have such an attentive
audience again. They listened with many a
hearty, if rough, expression of loyalty to the stars
and stripes and many equally hearty threats for

* This was the nickname of Colonel Caldwell's First Delaware Regiment in the
Revolutionary War. The original "blue hen" was the mother of a famous breed
of fighting gamecocks. Later the name was applied to the inhabitants of the whole
State.

the traitors. There seemed to be but one sentiment before the mast on board the " Wakulla," but,
as I found afterward, the quarter-deck and the
wardroom were not so unanimous.

Lieutenant Rogers and I went back to the " Constitution," he seemingly in a very thoughtful frame
of mind and I in a high state of elation. I
chattered away to him, boy like, about my experience among the rough sailor men on the
forecastle, and he listened rather absently, thinking, no doubt, of the puzzling questions that had
got to be worked out in the near future among the
officers.

" Your audience was better than mine," he said
sadly, after awhile, and when, in my enthusiasm, I
proposed to ship on board the " Wakulla," he shook
his head rather doubtfully, as if he thought I
might make a better selection. I had, however,
ascertained that she was short of boys when I was
on board, so, as she must of necessity be detained
a few days at Newport, I telegraphed to Stonyhaven, and my guardian came over on the next
train in answer to my summons.

To him I confided my wishes, and he held a
council of war with Mr. Rogers, after which they
went on board the " Wakulla," not taking me
with them, much to my chagrin; but at length

it was decided that I might as well make my
plunge into the service now as at any time. So
the requisite papers were executed by Captain
Shumway, as my guardian, and when the ship
was ready to sail I went on board and duly
signed articles. My kit consisted of a canvas
hammock, a pair of blankets, and a change of
clothing such as I had been accustomed to wear
ever since my introduction to the "Constitution."

"You'll find the fo'castle a rougher world than
my cabin, Jack," said Mr. Rogers, as he wrung
my hand and said good-by. "But you won't mind
as soon as you get used to it."

So that night I slung my new hammock for the
first time between decks, and went to sleep watching fifty or a hundred other similar hammocks
swing lazily to and fro, as the old sloop of war
surged out to sea under easy sail between Block
Island and Montauk Point, bound for Philadelphia.

I suppose never a boy entered the United States
service under better auspices than I. Ordinarily,
they are thrown in among the rough elements of a
ship's crew with small ceremony. Indeed, there
was not the least ceremony in my case. But yet
my circumstances were exceptional. Every man
on board knew me at sight as the youngster who
had delivered an impromptu lecture on secession.

I found myself quickly surrounded by friends, and, with very few exceptions, all continued to treat me well. The boys of my own age were not so kind, and I presently found out that if I would retain my self-respect I must fight without gloves. I may say that I did not altogether disgrace my record, as established at Annapolis, and after one or two of the larger boys had tried it on I was treated with due respect.

The "Wakulla" was only a moderately fast sailer, and three days after dropping Montauk Light we were still out of sight of land. About this time I began to notice a certain seriousness of deportment among the older seamen and warrant officers. It was an undefinable something that seemed to pervade the atmosphere of the ship fore and aft. Men looked askance at each other. The marines kept together at their own section of the main deck. Nothing was said apparently, and yet as the afternoon of the third day drew to a close I think there was not a soul on board that did not know something was wrong. I had not as yet formed any very intimate friendships, and could not expect to be treated with confidence by any of my shipmates. Therefore, it was with a certain unsatisfied and anxious curiosity that I turned into my hammock that night.

The steady roll of the ship, the swish of the water along the side, which I could hear through the open port, came drowsily to my ears, and before long I felt myself dropping off to sleep. But just at the last moment of consciousness a murmur of voices near at hand aroused me. By straining eyes and ears, I recognized the sergeant of marines and two or three gunners and quartermasters standing near the port at the foot of my hammock. Now any intimacy or intercourse between blue-jackets and marines is contrary to all precedent on board a man-of-war. Indeed, if any great cordiality should exist between the two grades the marine corps might as well be dispensed with altogether, for they are depended upon to make arrests among the crew, to maintain discipline in case of need, and to stand between the quarter-deck and the fo'castle in case of anything so serious as mutiny. I was wide awake in a moment, my curiosity instantly aroused by this evidently secret consultation. By dint of cautiously turning a bit in my blanket whenever the ship rolled, I was able to assume a posture where I could see and hear better.

"Sure, it's true what I'm telling you, sergeant," one of the quarter-masters was saying. "The wind's been nor' and west ever since we dropped

Montauk, and instead of giving us a course sou'-
west by west, which ought to have picked us up
the Delaware Capes by now, the ole man is giving her southing enough to clear Hatteras and run
us over Charleston bar before we know what's up.
You know what that means, — good-by, Uncle
Sam. I don't guess they'd hurt us much, but
they'd freeze onto the old ' Wakulla ' and all her
outfit, you can bet your life."

The sergeant was a man of few words and slow
of speech withal. He stood silent for awhile.
" You may be right, quarter-master," he said at
length. " I aint sayin' you're wrong; I ain't no
navigator myself, but it 'ud be mutiny, quarter-
master, to go agin' him. It 'ud be straight mutiny,
sure."

" I'm as much agin mutiny as you be, sergeant,
but I axes you what would it be if the ole man
should carry the ship into Charleston and hand
her over to the State of South Carolina? Would
that be 'mutiny or wot? Mutiny agin Uncle Sam,
for instance?"

The sergeant shook his head and said nothing;
evidently so profound a problem in political
ethics had never before been presented for his consideration.

" No," resumed the quarter-master, his voice

getting a bit shaky, " it wouldn't be mutiny, sergeant, but I'll tell you what it would be; it would be TREASON, that's what it would be."

The rest of the members of the little group nodded their heads, and I could hear them say in whispered tones, " That's so, sergeant; no more nor less than treason."

" It's hard lines for an old sergeant of marines," he said at length musingly. " I've always obeyed orders whether I liked them or not."

" So have I," broke in the more reckless sailor-man; " but you mark my words, Sergeant Jones, this here ship never gits across Charleston bar."

There was more talk of the same nature before the conspirators dispersed, and I lay awake an hour or more, dimly aware that something untoward was going on around me: dark figures flitted from one part of the 'tween decks 'to another, as if men were consulting together on the sly. But at last drowsiness asserted itself and I went off to sleep, only to be awakened when the watch was called in the morning.

The wind had changed during the night, and sunrise of the fourth day found it blowing from the southwest and we heading northwest on the port tack. As I went on deck, I was conscious of the same atmosphere of suppressed excitement prevailing among all hands. I was told that we had been heading in this direction since midnight, but no land was in sight, and no one seemed to know exactly where we were.

It was the custom on board this ship to have boys take their trick at the wheel under proper supervision in moderate weather, and it chanced that I was on duty there when the meridian observation was taken. Three officers "took the sun," as usual, reported eight bells, and went below to work up the ship's position. Presently two of them came on deck again, and I saw them exchange a quick, significant glance. They compared their figures, which apparently agreed, and the customary entry was duly made in the logbook. Then the navigating officer went below to report to the captain, who presently came on deck.

The two officers saluted and vacated the weather side for Captain Randall, who, barely acknowledging the salute, fell into a mechanical walk back and forth the length of the clear space between the quarter-bits and the break in the deck. He was a tall, dark-faced man, an excellent officer in every professional sense, but, as I have before said, a Southerner, and one of the proudest and bitterest of his class.

The second in command, Lieutenant Selden,

was, on the contrary, a New Englander by birth,
and every bit as proud of his birthplace and of
his family as was Randall himself.   The two
had been good enough friends, as friendships go
among naval officers on a long cruise, but the
.denouement at Newport had rather strained the
relations of the cabin and wardroom all round,
and it was whispered about the ship that of late
there had been some pretty plain talk between the
seniors in the seclusion of the captain's cabin and
arguments on the political situation that made
matters rather uncomfortable.   Before the mast,
of course, we had our own disputes and opinions,
but there was almost no disloyalty to the flag.

While this little tableau was arranging itself on
the quarter-deck the ship silently forged ahead
under all plain sail, dipping over the long rollers
with every inch of canvas drawing, and the great
white pyramid of lofty sails swaying gently to and
fro across the blue sky.

From my place at the wheel I could watch all
this display from the main truck to the foot of the
foresail, with the keen enjoyment of a sailor boy
who had not as yet known enough sea service to
be tired of it.   My companion and sponsor at the
wheel was one of the quarter-masters whom I had
overheard talking patriotic mutiny the night before

near my hammock, and it was evident to me that
he was in a state of deep, though suppressed, excitement. Indeed, the air of suspense to which I have
referred as pervading the whole ship's company
had rather increased than diminished during the
night.

The watch on deck was for the most part walking back and forth in couples or busied about
some kind of rigging or other ship's work. It
seemed to me, however, that rather an unusual
number of the off-duty men were on deck, and,
indeed, this afterward proved to be the case.

Half an hour or so passed in almost absolute
silence. Randall continued his walk, stopping now
and then to scan intently the horizon to windward.
At length he seemed to have made up his mind to
something, for he stopped half way in his walk aft
between the gangway and the bits, went forward,
and hailed the officer of the deck.

" Is there a lookout aloft, Mr. Fraser? "

" Yes, sir."

" Where is he?" (For the sails shut off his
view of the foremast.)

" In the foretopmast cross-trees, sir."

" Send him up to the royal yard."

" Very good, sir."

A pause of five minutes ensued while this order

was carried out. Then there was a hail from
aloft, but we could not make out the words on the
quarter-deck.

" What does he say, Mr. Fraser?" asked Randall, in the gangway.

" He reports something nearly abeam, sir, but
he can't make out whether it's a sail or a lighthouse."

Here the quarter-master whispered to me, " Now,
then, young 'un, if anything happens to take me
away from the wheel, you just stick to it, and keep
her full as she goes."

I suppose I must have looked rather wonderingly
at him, but he nodded encouragingly, hitched up
his trousers, sailor fashion, and felt inside the
bosom of his jacket with his right hand. As he
withdrew his hand I caught the gleam of something that looked very much like the butt of a
revolver. I will not deny that I began to wish I
was safe at Rockledge. Excitement, and fighting,
and boat expeditions, and so on were one thing,
but this dreadful suspense, and not knowing what
was the matter,— for nobody thought it would do to
trust a boy with a secret — was something terrible.

I noticed now that several of the other officers,
including Lieutenant Selden, had come on deck.
Going forward, he joined the officer on duty amid-

ships, and the two walked back and forth together.
At an ordinary time these little incidents would
have made no impression on my mind, but now
everything seemed to have a suggestive significance,
and around it all the calm summer sea, blue and
sparkling, and not a sail in sight, but beyond that
horizon to the westward of us we knew that nearly
half the territory of our country was in avowed
rebellion against the government to which we all
owed allegiance. What plots and counterplots were
hatching there for our capture we could not tell.

Presently Randall addressed one of the junior
officers on duty. "Coles," he said, "will you
oblige me by going aloft with the glass, and see
what you can make of it?"

"Certainly, sir." And Coles, who was an
active young fellow, went aloft like a topman, and
presently reported, "It's Hatteras Light, sir, sure
enough. I can see the keeper's house now."

"Very good, sir; you may come down. Stand
by to tack ship, Mr. Fraser."

Now every officer on deck and a good many of
the men who had an intelligent comprehension of
the state of things knew what this order meant,—
namely, Charleston and a surrender of the ship
and her crew to the Confederate authorities. This
did not dawn upon me at first. Then it suddenly

flashed upon me that we were heading almost in the direction of the Delaware Capes. We had sighted Hatteras, which was, so to speak, the turning point between North and South. To go about on the other tack meant that the captain had made up his mind to run for Charleston; a cold shiver ran down my back as I realized this.

My quarter-master gripped the spoke of the wheel with a hand that visibly trembled, and, although he did not speak audibly, I was in momentary terror lest he should draw his revolver and shoot down the captain where he stood.

As it turned out, however, there was no danger of this. The program had been too well arranged by the cool, loyal heads that had had the matter in charge. In pursuance of the order, the boatswain piped stations and the watch stood by tacks and sheets and manned the braces.

"Give her a good full."

"Ay, ay, sir."

"All ready there?"

"All ready, sir."

"Hard a lee then."

The quarter-master and I simultaneously threw our weight on the wheel to put the helm down, but not an inch would it budge. After one or two ineffectual efforts he sung out: —

"Wheel's jammed, sir."

"As you go, then. Mr. Selden, see if you can find out what's the matter."

Selden came up the gangway. His face was very pale, but he did not flinch. Walking straight up to Randall and standing close to him, he touched his cap in due form, and said very slowly and distinctly : —

"The wheel is jammed, Captain Randall."

"Yes, I know that; go and get it cleared."

"The — wheel — is — jammed, — sir ! "

I will not repeat here the precise language that Captain Randall used at this juncture. Suffice it to say that it was fluent and expressive. Selden heard him through, standing before him, and repeated : —

" *The wheel is jammed, sir.*"

At this, Randall, literally livid with rage, faced about, and glanced into the waist of the ship. The entire crew had assembled on deck without orders, — rather an unusual proceeding on board a man-of-war. Randall paled a little, but summoned the orderly who was on duty.

"Tell all officers to report on deck at once."

The orderly disappeared, and within a few seconds several of the junior officers were at their respective stations.

"Where are Simonds, and Travers, and the rest?" said Randall impatiently.

Selden was still standing near him. He had regained his usual demeanor now.

"The wheel is jammed, Captain Randall," he said again and he could not quite disguise a certain exultation in his tone. Randall was a brave and passionate man, but he knew when he was beaten, and, with marvelous coolness, accepted the situation.

"Mr. Fraser," he said, advancing to the gang-way, "there seems to be something the matter with the steering gear; loose the headsails if she pays off too much, and keep her on her course for the present. Mr. Selden, will you come below with me?"

As the two officers disappeared down the after companionway I think nearly every one on deck drew a sigh of relief, and there was a little grumble of congratulation, not unmingled with threats, passed among them as the off-duty men began to go below, while the watch on deck coiled away the running rigging.

At this moment I was aware, partly through my grip on the wheel spokes and partly through the evidence of my ears, of a certain clanking, as of a chain being overhauled. Presently the wheel surged naturally to the lift of the sea, the compass

card slowly revolved till the "lubber's mark"
touched N. W. by N., the weather leech of the
topsail shook a little, and the quarter-master winked
profoundly at me and thrust his tongue into his
cheek as two men came aft to relieve us.

Everybody felt that a grave crisis was safely
passed, but very few knew that a certain volunteer
from among the ship's boys had been slung over
the stern in a bowline an hour or two before, and
had temporarily shortened the rudder chain pend-
ants with a rope seizing, so that, while the helm was
available for ordinary steering, it could not be put
"hard over" until the seizing was cast off.

What passed between Randall and Selden at
their interview in the cabin none of us blue-
jackets ever knew, but they both came on deck
after an hour or so, and walked amicably together
while the watch was changing at eight bells that
afternoon. Nothing more was said about tacking
ship, and as the wind held from the southwest,
we made the Virginia capes before morning, and
forty-eight hours later were safe inside the breakwater and running up the Delaware between the
loyal States of Pennsylvania and New Jersey.

For the benefit of landsmen, it should, perhaps,
be explained here that mutiny on ship board,
even in the merchant service, is punishable with

death.　In the navy, where discipline is far stricter, every man knows that he takes his life in his hand if he ventures to defy his superior. The loyal officers of the " Wakulla," therefore, showed a high quality of courage when they conspired together to save the ship to the government to which they owed allegiance. Secession was not even branded as a punishable offense. Officers in the military service of the United States had willingly— nay, eagerly— surrendered ships, forts, and public property, and were not even censured by the Department.

Such were the doubts and distrust that unavoidably prevailed at Washington under conditions that had never been foreseen that peace on some terms was still among the possibilities, and there was no telling what might happen to officers who interpreted maritime law according to their own personal views and in defiance of what was certainly established authority at the time.

Never, I suppose, was a revolt on the high seas and its suppression conducted so systematically as was this one on the Wakulla. Not a single mutinous word was spoken aloud from beginning to end. The nearest approach to it was Selden's reiterated assertion that the wheel was " jammed," but that could hardly have been construed as actual mutiny. It is a question for sea lawyers to wrangle over, whether, under such unprecedented circumstances, treason was intended on one side and mutiny justifiable on the other.

If the senior officer had not been cool-headed enough to see that the game was lost he would, without question, have been seized and put in irons. That this would have been rank mutiny goes without saying, and it will never be known what a court-martial would have done in such a case. No doubt Selden expressed this to his commander in a friendly way during their interview in the cabin, and, no doubt, he explained, too, why the Southern officers on whose help Randall had relied had not found it altogether convenient to obey when they were ordered on deck.

On our arrival at Philadelphia, the Southerners promptly resigned their commissions, the only honorable step open to them under the circumstances, and took service at once with the Confederacy.

There was a general paying off and dispersion of the crew on our arrival at the navy yard. But most of them re-enlisted for the war after a few days, having gotten rid of their money in the meantime, with the traditional facility of sailor men. Some few of my mates, however, who, for some reason or other, had nowhere to go and no inclination to squander their savings, shouldered their canvas bags with me and went over to the receiving ship that lay alongside the wharf.

This was an old dismantled three-decker that had been lying in the mud off League Island from time immemorial. She afforded comfortable quarters, however, for recruits, and we were soon assigned messes during our stay. I was presently drafted, and assigned to a small coasting steamer that had just been purchased for the government and was in process of conversion into a gunboat for blockading and reconnoitering duty down the coast.

She was named the " Otter," and carried two four-inch pivot rifles, one forward and the other aft, with four howitzers amidships, two on a side. All four of these, however, could be brought into battery on either side in case of need. Although she was still in the hands of riggers and ship carpenters when we went on board, I could see that she had ship-shape possibilities. We of the new draft dumped our kits in the wake of the windlass, where they were out of the way, and patiently awaited developments.

Everything was in confusion on board, in consequence of the land-lubberly ways of the workmen and mechanics, but your true sailor man has a certain compassionate pity for fellow mortals who are not bred to the sea, so we sat around and contented ourselves with ridiculing these honest fellows who were fitting up our future home for us. I am bound to say that they gave back as good as they received, so that in the end we became fairly good friends. In the course of the day, we somehow got our mess assignments, and wrote our names or made our marks in the ship's book according to the degree of our literary accomplishments.

The work of bolting down traverse circles, fitting hatches, reenforcing timbers, and the like went on by shifts day and night, and, finding that there would be no such thing as sleep for me if I remained on board, I proposed to another boy with whom I had already fraternized that we should slip ashore and camp among some ship's stores that lay under a shed a little way back from the wharf.

Amid the prevailing bustle it was not difficult for us to swing ourselves down to the wharf, and then, watching our chance when the guard was looking the other way, to slip under the dark shadow of the shed. Here we soon found a comfortable retreat among certain bales of blankets, and slept the sleep of youth and innocence, in

defiance of naval regulations and of the noisy
hammers of the workmen who made night hideous
on board the " Otter." I, at least, was totally unconscious until daylight, when, by the merest good
luck, my companion awoke just in time to learn
from the bustle that he could hear outside that the
" Otter " was actually casting off her lines preparatory to departure.

We made a desperate run for it, and succeeded
in scrambling aboard by the chains before she
swung clear of the wharf. The gang of mechanics, it appeared, was to accompany her down the
river, to be brought back by the tug, such was the
haste, in those early days of the war, with which
vessels were equipped for service. It was no unusual thing to start on a voyage without knowing
whether the engines would work or not. No
elaborate trial trips were possible over measured
miles, and with a small squadron of tenders and
time-keepers. As likely as not, a trial trip in 1861
might end under the guns of a rebel battery or on
some blockading station where fire rafts and
cutting-out expeditions were among possibilities by
no means remote.

In reality, however, the work was pretty well
along in our case before we started, and when we
reached the Delaware breakwater that afternoon

there were only the finishing touches to be added. The engineer had gotten up steam on the way down, and the last twenty miles we had run with our own machinery. Everything appeared to work so well and the night promised to be so calm that it was decided to send the workmen back on the tug and put to sea at once. Accordingly, the regular watches were told off, the decks were swept, and just before sunset the little " Otter" rounded the breakwater, pointed her nose to the South, and began to rise and fall regularly on the Atlantic swells.

From Delaware Bay to the Chesapeake is only a hundred and fifty miles, but our engines had been largely made over, and, like all new machinery, must be treated with much tenderness. We proceeded, therefore, under easy steam, the engineers having orders to take no risks, and by afternoon of the next day entered Hampton Roads.

CHAPTER VII.

THE OTTER'S FIRST PRIZE.

THE mouth of Chesapeake Bay in the vicinity of Fortress Monroe assumed great importance as soon as hostilities fairly began. The proclamation of the blockade naturally brought together a considerable fleet in Hampton Roads, and the near vicinity of the navy yard at Norfolk, now in Confederate hands, and of Richmond, shortly to be the Confederate capital, rendered it necessary to maintain a considerable force at that point. As we came up to our anchorage, we could see the rebel flag flying over a newly erected earthwork, just out of range on our port bow, but on the opposite shore the stars and stripes floated over the grim fortress and over extensive camps beyond, which showed that the North was responding in earnest to the president's call for troops. We let go the anchor and reported to the flagship, Captain Ross, no doubt, explaining how we had left Philadelphia with workmen on board, and had hastened our departure to such a degree that it would take us, at least, twenty-four hours to finish getting to rights.

Commodore Stringham, an officer of the old navy, was at this time in command of the "North Atlantic" Squadron, having charge nominally of the entire coast. At this time, only a few days after the proclamation, he had not been able to enforce the blockade with any degree of stringency, and it was necessary, besides, for him to retain a sufficient fleet to meet emergencies at Hampton Roads itself. His flagship was the fine steam frigate, "Minnesota."

After leaving us the needed time to complete our repairs, that is to say until afternoon of the day following, the old gentleman came alongside in his twelve-oared barge, and was piped up the gangway in as good shape as we could manage with our new crew. He had us called to quarters, and looked us over from the battery to magazine, asking shrewd, seaman-like questions about our draught, and how much coal we carried, and all the rest.

As he passed my station in company with the captain, I overheard the latter ask him : —

"May I make a little trial trip to-morrow, commodore? I'd like to see if the machinery works all right at full speed."

Permission was granted, but the commodore added : —

"Don't start till I signal you about it. I may want to have you go in some particular direction."

The next morning, about ten o'clock, our number went fluttering up to the peak of the flagship with a string of colored pennants below it, which read, "Captain, come aboard flagship."

The gig was called away, and, as I was told off as bow boy in the captain's crew, I swung myself down from the boom into my place; the oarsmen followed, and in a moment we were skimming away over the dimpling water toward the big flag-ship.

The "Minnesota" was one of five screw frigates that were finished shortly before the Civil War. They were probably the finest vessels of their kind ever built anywhere, outmatching vessels of their class in all the navies of Europe. They were rated at about thirty-five hundred tons displacement, and carried fifty-two guns of the heaviest calibre then in use afloat. They were the last of their type, for "iron pots" were just coming in, and fighting navies had no further use for wooden walls.

I had been watching this magnificent ship ever since we anchored at a little distance from her, but

I had no conception of her size until a nearer approach. As we rounded to by the starboard gangway and I caught the mooring ring with my boathook, it seemed to me that we were alongside a veritable floating fortress, the long range of black muzzled cannon protruding from the open ports, the massive curving sides, topped with a row of white hammocks, and over all the slender lofty spars, draped at this moment with canvas shaken out to dry, all combined to impress me with a feeling very akin to awe.

I could dimly remember a somewhat similar sensation when, as a child of tender years, my father took me on board the "Molly Pitcher," and again when, a brief two months before, I had, for the first time, climbed the side of the old "Constitution."

But here surely was a ship invincible. I would have matched her against anything afloat without a moment's hesitation. Indeed, I was not far out in my estimate of her powers, though I little thought that in less than a year from that very time I should see her at the mercy of her once sister ship, the "Merrimac," then lying in the mud at Norfolk navy yard, hardly a dozen miles distant.

We of the crew sat in the boat speculating as to the fighting power of the "Minnesota," while the

captain went up the gangway to report.   He was
detained only a few minutes, and presently came
down again in lively fashion, looking as happy as
a boy with a holiday in prospect, and gave orders
to pull back to the " Otter."

Of course he did not say a word to any of his
boat's crew ; that wouldn't have been etiquette, but
no sooner had he disappeared on deck than the
boatswain piped " All boats aboard," and while
we were making fast the falls we could hear the
clank of the windlass for'ard as the cable was hove
short.

The boats were all at the davits in a few minutes,
and then came the cry, " Man the starboard gangway," and presently Commodore Stringham, the
flag officer, came aboard with one of his staff.
He had the confidence, I think, of his entire command, and after leading his fleet to the first con-
spicuous success of the war on land or sea,
every one thought that he was the coming man as a
naval commander, but, for some reason or other,
he was shelved by the Department and given an
inglorious command on shore duty.

" No, captain, you needn't set my flag," I heard
him say as he walked forward.   " I'll just go along
as a passenger.   Run her out past the Capes and
see how she takes the sea."

So the anchor was catted; the captain started
easy, but presently gave her " four bells," the signal for full speed, for the first time since leaving
Philadelphia, and we went spinning out past the
grim, gray fortress, and out between the Capes
half a dozen miles to sea.   The engines had to be
stopped once or twice on account of heated jour-
nals, but this was no more than was to be expected,
and, upon the whole, for a makeshift gunboat she
behaved admirably.

Returning, we ran through the fleet, and headed
for the mouth of James River, Sewell's Point
taking a crack at us as we steamed past, but the
shot mostly fell short or went wide of us, so we
took no notice whatever, but went on up the river
toward Richmond till it narrowed so that it was
hardly safe to proceed farther.

Richmond was not as yet the capital of the Confederacy, and the banks of the James had not yet
echoed to the sound of contending armies. All
was as peaceful, save for certain uncompleted
earthworks that we passed, as it had been since
the first settlers came in and made themselves
homes along its fertile shores.

As a New England boy, I knew that two of the
very earliest settlements on the shores of this
Western Continent had contained the elements of

discord that were just now bearing fruit in civil war. My own home was not far from where a little band had landed with freedom and liberty for its watchword. Here, on the contrary, I found myself in sight of the first settlement where negro slavery was brought to the shores of America, and I looked upon it from the deck of a gunboat prepared to defend the nation against a rebellion, the strength of which was not as yet realized.*

Of course, I did not formulate all this even in my own mind, but I think I dimly realized the significance of it all, and determined to do my duty though I was only a " powder monkey."

After going as far as was deemed prudent, and making no discoveries of importance, we returned to our anchorage. Our friends on the Point were ready for us as we came back, seeming desirous, apparently, of expending their ammunition on the slightest possible pretext. A few days afterward the Richmond papers referred to the affair as one which reflected unbounded credit upon the artillerists, a formidable naval attack having been beaten off and the enemy compelled to withdraw, apparently in a disabled condition. Such exaggerated accounts of trifling affairs of this character were far too common on both sides during the early days

* See note at end of the chapter.

of the war, when neither side knew what serious work really meant, and every editor considered it his duty to encourage the volunteers to the extent of his ability, regardless of the truth.

This little picnic excursion we soon found had been undertaken by the commodore in order to satisfy himself regarding our state of discipline and efficiency for more important service. Seemingly he was fairly well satisfied with the performance, for we had been able to show him a speed of twelve or fifteen knots an hour, which was pretty well for a gunboat in those days.

As a crew we had hardly as yet settled down to good naval form, but Captain Ross was well known to be a good disciplinarian and a good commander, so, as he was lucky enough to have the most efficient light draught gunboat that had as yet joined the fleet, we of the crew thought we were pretty certain to see some active service before long.

Sure enough, we received orders the next day to take on all the coal we could make room for, and closely following this came the orders to sail. Precisely what these instructions were nobody save the captain knew, but there was general rejoicing that, at least, we were not going to be kept indefinitely lying in the inglorious security of Hampton Roads.

As soon as it was dark enough to hide our movements from the enemy's lookout on Sewell's Point we got under way as silently as possible, and stood out to sea, turning to the southward. It was with something of nervousness, hardly acknowledged to myself, that I watched the light on Cape Charles sink out of sight astern. South of this not a single lighthouse, so far as we knew, now sent out its friendly beams over the desolate sea. The Confederates had extinguished them all as soon as the acts of secession were passed.

Often they had wantonly smashed the costly refracting lanterns, and destroyed the complicated machinery, apparently for no reason excepting that there was no one to prevent them from doing it. In one or two instances the lighthouse keepers had made a show of opposition, and in one case, at least (at Cape Canaveral), the lantern and its belongings were carried away and hidden by the keeper and saved from certain destruction. It should be said, however, that this was not done from any sense of loyalty to the United States, but simply because the keeper could not bear to have a fine piece of machinery destroyed for which he felt a certain personal attachment.

Keeping well off the coast, daylight found us off Cape Hatteras, and shortly afterward we were cautiously approaching Hatteras Inlet, twelve miles south of the cape, which was the principal navigable entrance to Pamlico Sound.

Here it was rumored that the rebels were erecting fortifications, and we cautiously sounded our way in, the captain conning the ship from the foremast crosstrees. Like a prudent navigator, he had consulted the nautical almanac before his arrival, and had timed it so as to make the bar when the tide was running flood. A long, smooth swell was bursting over bars and beaches, and even from the deck, as we drew in toward the land, we could judge the depth of the water by its color.

It was not the captain's intention, however, seriously to engage any fortifications or vessels that might be found here. His object was simply to reconnoiter, and we were all reasonably confident that we had the heels of anything at that time floating the Confederate flag.

Any one who will take the trouble to look at a map of the North Atlantic coast must be forcibly impressed by the ingratitude of the republic to beneficent nature. Almost the entire coast from the Chesapeake to the extremity of Florida is adapted by nature to encourage the pursuit of commerce, and yet this great and intelligent republic has not taken advantage of it even to this very day.

All along this stretch of coast a succession of
outlying bars, and islands, and peninsulas lies a
few miles or a few rods off the mainland, forming
sheltered sounds and estuaries near a thousand
miles in extent. On one side the wild Atlantic
thunders ceaselessly in storm and calm ; on the
other side peaceful waters lap the sand and storm-
driven coasters find a safe anchorage. These
sheltered sounds are connected with the ocean by
numerous inlets which vary in depth, according to
the force and direction of the wind, the state of
the tide, the outflow of fresh water, and a hundred
other conditions that combine to puzzle the enterprising navigator.

The Confederate authorities were prompt to
recognize the importance of fortifying the more
considerable of these inlets, and no sooner had
the rich prize of the Norfolk Navy Yard fallen into
their hands than they set about transporting guns
and war material to Hatteras and Okracoke Inlets.
The first named of these is only a few miles south
of the stormy cape from which it takes its name,
and, although its habits in the matter of shifting
sands and the like are very irregular, still they are
far more regular than those of its fellows. Indeed,
it is the most accessible of any of the entrances to
the North Carolina sounds.

Hatteras Inlet has an outer bar rather more than a mile from the beach, with about fourteen feet of water at high tide. Then there is an inner bar known as the Bulkhead, which, at ordinary tides, has only about seven feet of water. From these depths it would appear that only small vessels can find their way in and out, but with the south-easterly winds which are of quite frequent occurrence, the water, in some mysterious way, banks up over these bars, until large vessels, under skilful pilotage, can make their way in and out without danger. Over either of these bars we, with our light draught, could pass with impunity, and in the comparatively quiet water between the two could make our observations without danger from hostile guns.

At this time the privateers and blockade runners were having it all their own way in the North Carolina sounds, and Hatteras Inlet afforded them their principal means of egress and entry. Quite a number of coasting vessels had already been captured by Confederate privateers, and British blockade runners were already beginning to perceive the opportunity that was opening for them. A small fleet was anchored inside the beach, while we could see a considerable force of men at work, apparently throwing up fortifications on both sides of the inlet.

Running in within easy range, we gave them a few shots from our bow rifle, not with the intention of doing any damage, but in order to invite a reply in kind, so that we could learn the calibre and range of their artillery. Some old hand was apparently in charge, however, for as soon as the first shell was fired the men took to cover and only showed themselves long enough to induce us to fire again. No heavy guns were as yet ready for service.

So, after getting as good an idea as possible of the intended works, we steamed away down to Okracoke, eighteen miles away, and repeated our investigations in that vicinity. Nothing was doing there, and by mid-afternoon we were re-passing Hatteras on our return northward, when a sail was reported in the offing, and a few minutes' observation showed that she was standing in for the inlet.

Our course was altered at once so as to intercept her and ascertain her character, for if she should prove to be a blockade runner it was well to have her as far from her friends as possible, and if she should be a privateer, why, then our chances would be so much the better in the open sea. In an hour we were able to make her out as a large brigantine pretty well down in the water and, therefore, probably not a privateer. We set our ensign and rounded to, indicating a wish to communicate. She showed English colors and kept on her way. We then fired the customary gun, but Johnny Bull took no notice; upon which we gave him a solid shot across his bows, which convinced him that we meant business. Accordingly, the English captain threw his foreyard aback, and stood at the taffrail bellowing something through a speaking trumpet, but he was to leeward and we could not hear what he said, except that it sounded very much as if he was in a great state of rage. So Captain Ross sent a boat with an officer to examine his papers. In a few minutes he returned, reporting that it was a clear case of blockade running, the Englishman having sailed from Bermuda with a contraband cargo for one of the North Carolina ports, and with full knowledge of the president's blockade proclamation.

"He says," added the lieutenant, "that the blockade is nothing but paper, anyway, and he is going on as soon as he gets ready."

Sure enough, the men were already hauling her head sails to windward, preparatory to filling the brigantine away again on her course.

Captain Ross now hailed from the bridge. We had drifted nearer together. "This is the United

States blockading steamer ' Otter.' Heave to or I'll fire into you."

" This is the British brigantine ' Argo.' Fire if you dare."

Captain Ross spoke to his lieutenant, who went to one of the broadside guns. " Let him have it through the foresail, gunner; don't damage his spars if you can help it; fire as she rises."

The gunner sighted carefully, and as she rose on a second roll pulled his lanyard. A big rent appeared in the square foresail of the brigantine.

" Is that enough?" Ross hailed from the bridge.

" No, you Yankee pirate, it ain't enough, and you'll sweat for this," the Englishman replied, with considerable unnecessary language in addition, which I will not here repeat.

By this time the brigantine had gained some headway, and we had rounded to nearly alongside of her, keeping pace with her under easy steam.

" Look here," said Captain Ross, keeping his temper and hailing again. " Don't you see that I can blow you out of the water in two minutes, if I choose? Throw your ship up in the wind, or take the consequences."

The Englishman looked forward at his split foresail and glanced at the guns that were trained upon him, and decided that, after all, it looked as though the blockade was something more than a paper one. So he concluded to obey orders, and brought his vessel into the wind again, while preparations were hastily made on the "Otter" to send a prize crew on board and start the captured vessel for New York.

NEGRO SLAVERY. In August, 1619, a Dutch warship arrived at Jamestown, Virginia, with twenty African negroes, whom the settlers bought, and they became bondmen. Thus was slavery established at the South. In 1646 the General Court of Massachusetts sent back to their native land two Africans who had been captured in a slave hunt, and pronounced "man stealing" a capital offense. Thus was the idea of equal rights for all affirmed at the North. So profitable was the slave trade, however, that England insisted that slavery should be recognized as lawful in all her American colonies, and so it remained until independence was achieved, when the Northern States, led by Vermont, began to pass laws for its suppression. The Southern idea was that certain human creatures might properly be held in perpetual bondage, while the Northern theory pronounced all men — including negroes — free and equal. With these irreconcilable ideas as to human rights, the two sections, North and South, grew until they began to crowd one another, and each insisted that the other should adopt its ideas. Neither would yield, and the question had to be settled by war. The North won, being richer and stronger than the South, and so, in 1863, the slaves were emancipated by President Lincoln, and the doctrine of equal rights, as declared by Plymouth Colony in 1620, became the law of the whole land.

CHAPTER VIII.

A RUNNING FIGHT.

A DOZEN men were hastily told off, and one of the junior officers detailed to take the prize to New York. Even a man-o'-wars man needs a few minutes to pack when ordered to change his quarters, and while the men were hastily thrusting a change of clothing into canvas bags, and throwing the latter into the boat that was already alongside, the lookout hailed : —

" Two steamers coming out of the inlet, sir."

We had run out so far from land to meet our prize that the low coast line was now invisible from the deck, and we could see only two feathery lines of smoke in the direction from which we had come. Captain Ross sprang into the rigging with his glass, and by going half way up to the mast-head was able to make out two river craft, side wheelers, just crossing the bulkhead.

Black smoke was pouring from their funnels, and they straightway headed up the coast with the apparent intention of cutting us off from our recently captured prize. Jacky is, or always should be, ready for a fight, but he is peculiarly pugnacious in temperament when what he regards as rightfully earned prize money is in danger. None of us knew, of course, the value of the brigantine's cargo, but it did not lose anything in our estimation on that account.

It was enough that we had gathered that this cargo was in the main composed of war material destined for the Confederacy, and war material in those days was worth a very pretty sum. At any rate, seventy-five or a hundred thousand dollars, divided among our crew of eighty men and boys, would not come amiss, and even if the sum total were considerably less than that it was at least worth fighting for. If we foremast hands had been consulted, I don't doubt but we should have voted unanimously to go about, meet the rebel craft half way, and sink them both, or be sunk ourselves before another hour had passed.

Fortunately, the commanders of United States vessels are usually possessed of cooler heads than are common between decks. When Captain Ross had finished his survey he replaced his marine glass in its leather case and swung himself down to the deck as coolly as if he had merely gone aloft to watch a school of porpoises play. He walked across to the side where the prize men were almost ready to shove off, with young Mr. Casey in the stern sheets.

"I meant to have a word with you, Casey, before you went," the captain called, as he leaned over the rail; "but no matter, I can tell you here just as well. Bend a new foresail as soon as you can, and square away for New York under everything she will carry. Keep well off shore to clear the shoals north of Cape Hatteras. If that English skipper cuts up rough, put him in irons without any hesitation."

Blue-jackets are not very often privileged to be present when private instructions are given to their official superiors. There were broad grins on the faces of the boat's crew, as well as on the long line of sun-burned countenances that hung over the "Otter's" rail. Jacky greatly relished summary measures with the captain of the prize.

"Very good, sir," Casey replied; "I'll see to it, sir. Shove off."

The men tossed their oars into the rowlocks; the heavily laden boat swung away from the side, and soon transferred its load to the prize. To pull back and be hoisted to its own davits was but the work of a few moments. The "Otter" had been practically cleared for action all day, so we had

nothing to do but to possess our souls in patience
and divide our time between watching the approach
of the steamers and commenting on the alacrity
with which young Casey made his presence felt on
board the " Argo."

We took position just under the lee of the prize,
so as to be at hand if anything happened, and were
so near that we could see and could even hear by
snatches everything that took place on her sloping
deck. The burly, red-faced skipper was walking
up and down on the quarter-deck, raging inwardly,
no doubt, at the indignity thus heaped upon him.

Young Casey had stationed two well-armed
Jackies aft with a third at the wheel to watch the
" old man," and had himself gone forward to see
if the new foresail was all right. That work was
well under way in charge of an old sailor man who
knew far more about bending sails then Casey
himself did, so he turned his attention to the somewhat sullen-looking group comprising the crew of
the brigantine, who had gathered on the forecastle,
neither helping nor hindering the work in hand.
To them Casey addressed himself; although the
distance was too great for us to hear his words, we
could understand pretty well what he was saying.
At any rate, the men listened and seemed to consult
among themselves quite earnestly as he walked aft.

Casey took the weather side of the deck, as a matter of course, the skipper continuing his wrathful walk and paying no attention whatever to the somewhat cockey youngster in blue uniform who was thus invading his domain. Presently Casey spoke to him, and he stopped abruptly in his walk, with indignation bristling from every hair of his head. He stood with his feet wide apart, sailor fashion, his arms akimbo, and his whole attitude expressive of outraged Insular dignity. Casey addressed a few words to him, and then began walking back and forth, as the skipper had walked before.

So far as I could hear, nothing further was said, but the skipper's face grew so much redder than before, as he stood rooted to the deck, that I expected to see him fall down in an apoplectic fit. Instead of this, however, after puffing out his cheeks for a moment, he mechanically took off his cap with his left hand, and began to rub the back of his head with his right. He continued doing this for fully two minutes, meanwhile watching Casey as if uncertain whether to throw him overboard or not. Then he suddenly clapped his hat on his head, and dived down the companionway into the cabin, whence, as we afterwards learned, he did not emerge till the "Argo" dropped anchor in New York Harbor.

Sympathetic grins and sundry appreciative winks were interchanged among the members of our crew. Casey was rather a favorite among us, and we were glad to see him establish his official standing as commander of the "prize"; not much danger, we thought, that the crew would be able to capture that vessel before she reached her destination. Casey stopped walking as soon as the captain was out of sight, looked at his watch, and hailed the forecastle.

"Time's up, men," he called. "Lay aft here."

The men slouched aft in a straggling procession, as ordered, and gathered in a group in front of the youthful prize-master. We could not hear what was said, but could see that Casey was talking to them in an earnest way, and, upon the whole, the interview seemed to be satisfactory. For, after an appeal to the men and a seeming motion of assent all round, he spoke loud enough for us to catch his reply.

"That's good; I am glad that you take a sensible view of the case. Many hands will make light work, and I should have been very sorry to have to put any of you in irons. Go forward now and get that foresail bent as soon as possible."

Then followed an interview with the mate and sub-officers of the brigantine, who apparently ex-

pressed their willingness to resume their old duties
so far as concerned their own men. All sail was
put on the brigantine, and on her decks affairs
settled down into the ordinary routine of a sailing
craft, save for the two or three armed blue-jackets
who were posted at certain points of the deck.

This little drama, seen rather than heard, was,
of course, a side issue, and, as I have said, divided
our time and served, perhaps, to steady our nerves
while we watched the hostile steamers come slowly
in sight, first showing their funnels and then their
hulls above the western horizon.

By this time they were in plain sight and overhauling us quite rapidly. The " Argo," however,
under her additional spread of sail, was now bowling along at a famous rate of speed, and we
sheered off across her wake to see if, perchance,
the enemy would follow us instead of her. But
they were not to be diverted. Seeing us head out
to sea, they drew together for a moment's consultation, and then both kept their course after the
" Argo." That, indeed, was the only reasonable
thing for them to do. The outcome of a fight
with us was at least doubtful, and if we were
afraid to defend our prize they might recapture
her with but little trouble. Anyhow, to fight us in
the vicinity of the prize would involve no more

risk than chasing us out to sea and taking their chances on blue water.

The "Otter's" policy, on the other hand, was to put off fighting as long as she could. Taking the two steamers separately, she could probably have made short work with either of them, barring accident, but together they were perhaps more than a match for her, because they could choose their own positions, and one of them, at least, would be certain to have a manifest advantage.

We could see by this time, even with the naked eye, that they both carried heavy guns forward, nine-inch dahlgrens, we thought they were, and lighter ones in broadside. It was astonishing in those days to see what tremendous guns were mounted for service in the shallow waters of the sound on flimsy little river craft that a regular artillery officer would say could not stand the recoil of anything heavier than a boat howitzer. Stand it they did, however, and throughout the four years while the blockade was maintained the great Carolina sounds were patrolled by little steamers carrying guns weighing almost as much as they weighed themselves.

Dropping half a mile astern of the "Argo," Captain Ross awaited developments. The enemy's craft separated and crept up, one on either side of

us; still, however, at a considerable distance.
The situation had changed a little by this, for the
"Argo" was now logging off eight knots or so
with a southeasterly breeze broad on her quarter.
The enemy could overhaul us but slowly at this
rate, and, as the sea was rising, it must have been
a question with them whether or not they had
better venture farther from shore.

They kept on, however, and we, purposely not
going so fast, diminished the gap between us and
our pursuers. I was, of course, wholly inexpe-
rienced in judging distances at sea, but I inferred
from the talk that went on around me that we
must be nearly within range. The crew of the
after-rifle were at their station, and Captain Ross
was watching the chase closely. At length, just
as it seemed to me that I could not possibly keep
still any longer, but must, at least, yell in my excitement, thereby committing a serious breach of discipline, he gave the order : --

"You may try the offshore one, now, Mr.
Bosworth."

The captain of the gun patted the breach of the
big rifle affectionately, the crew swung its muzzle
a little to starboard, and Bosworth, sighting with
one eye, seemed to watch the lift of the sea with
the other. Firing from a reeling deck at a distant

object that bobs up and down on the restless sea
is uncertain work at best; it calls for a rare combination of quickness of eye, of good judgment,
and of scientific accuracy.

The critical moment, of course, is the instant of
firing, and the gunner must anticipate by the frac-
tion of a second the probable movement of his gun
as the ship rises or falls on the heaving sea.
Experience and aptitude often develop a wonderful skill in ships' gunners; they seem to know by
instinct the curve that will be followed by the
muzzle of the gun as it sweeps up or down, below
and above the horizon. That this movement is
wholly beyond reach of accurate calculation must
be evident to any one who has watched the motions
of waves. It is bad enough with broadside guns,
but with a pivot rifle on the stern of a little screw
propeller the situation was much worse.

The "Otter" was kicking up her heels in a
rising sea, and old Bosworth must have been
much put to it. I watched him with intense interest, for I hoped some day to be a gunner
myself. He waited till he thought there was a
fair chance for a good combination of roll, lift,
and scend, then pulled the lanyard, and all hands
breathlessly watched to see where the shot would
strike. After what seemed a very long interval, a

column of spray shot up a little astern of the enemy.

"Very good for a first shot, Bosworth," said Captain Ross. "Load and fire at will now, and don't forget to give the inshore boat a taste of your metal as soon as you fairly get the range."

The enemy reserved his fire until he had drawn a little nearer, and then let fly a nine-inch solid shot, which, by a most extraordinary piece of good luck for him and bad luck for us, knocked off the corner of our after deckhouse, and smashed one of the quarter-boats into kindling wood. Fortunately, nobody was very seriously hurt, but I must admit that it gave me a bit of a turn to hear the roar of the shot overhead, and to see a man led below with a splinter slash across his forehead that filled his eyes with blood and left a ghastly train of red spots on the white deck behind him.

That first shot, however, was the beginning and end of their luck. They never touched us again, and although the exchange of shots was kept up till dusk in a leisurely way, it was at long range; no farther damage resulted to either side, so far as we knew.

Captain Ross, no doubt, wanted to come to closer quarters as much as the rest of us did, but I can see now that he was quite right not to take any chances at that time. As the sun sank behind the low-lying bank of Cape Hatteras our pursuers decided to give it up, and, with a parting shot at them as they presented their broadsides to us in turning, we quickened our pace, overtook and hailed the "Argo" before eight bells, and, finding all right on board, sheered off to complete our reconnaissance by an inspection of Roanoke Island, which, next to Hatteras Inlet, was regarded as the most important strategic point on the Carolina shore.

Standing off and on till daylight, we ran into Oregon Inlet, and speedily found that the island itself was quite beyond our reach, so far, at least, as concerned a satisfactory inspection. The inlet was so shallow that our small boats sent in to take soundings could hardly find water enough to float themselves across the bar. Moreover, quite a little fleet of steam and sailing craft lay at anchor within the bar, so that it would have been extremely rash for us to venture across.

We sent armed parties ashore, however, at a place called Nagg's Head, and succeeded in capturing some negro fishermen, by whom we were assured that no fortifications were as yet even begun on the island and that only a company or so of soldiers was quartered there. They told us,

however, that all the light-draught steamers to be
found on the sound had been armed and manned,
and were ready to pounce upon any incautious
coasting craft that came within reach.

This information was considered sufficient, so
we returned to Hampton Roads, well content with
the outcome of our first cruise, and very proud of
the performance of our little makeshift man-o'-war
" Otter."

I may say here, before dismissing the subject,
that the " Argo " reached New York safely, was
duly condemned by an admiralty court in the
presence of the British consul, who entered no
protest, and was eventually sold for $65,000, of
which my share, by some mysterious process of
arithmetic which I never could fathom, amounted
to $237.53, which was proudly placed to my credit
in Stonyhaven Savings Bank by my good Uncle
Abner as soon as received.

CHAPTER IX.

CONTRABAND OF WAR.

AFTER her return to Hampton Roads the "Otter" was used mainly as a despatch boat for awhile, and neither she nor any of her crew had any adventures worth speaking of until August. The time was passed mainly in drilling at the guns and in boat parties, which latter included landing and the management of the convenient little howitzers that were part of the outfit of every United States war vessel.

Commodore Stringham had for some time cherished a wish to attack and reduce, with the coöperation of the army, the fortifications at Hatteras Inlet, which we had been sent to inspect. The navy had from the first appreciated the strategic importance of this position, but had been unable to convince the army authorities.

During these early weeks of declared hostilities the contrast between the army and navy was rather painfully perceptible. From the nature of things, these two branches of the service were very different in their official organization. The army, having its stations in time of peace in comfortable quarters and on shore, was naturally under the control of senior officers, who were apt to be crotchety. Of late years this has been in a measure corrected, but at the time of the outbreak of the Civil War the army was notably weak in this respect.

A venerable officer, who had in his time done noteworthy service for his country, was summoned to Washington to superintend the organization of an army, the like of which had never entered into his wildest dreams. It did not seem possible to him and to the most trusted of his advisers to enter upon any undertaking of consequence without due preparation and without a large number of troops.

The navy, on the contrary, even in time of peace, is largely on active duty, that is to say, at sea. Its effective ships are always under the command of officers who expect to do their share of sea service. Its cruisers are constantly waging war against the elements in all seas. Its men are frequently exercised at the guns, and are almost invariably kept up to a high degree of efficiency. These facts, taken in connection with the far more complicated features of the political situation on land, conspired to induce a rather unusual degree of caution on the part of the army departments.

While the ships of the navy, at the outbreak of hostilities, had been widely scattered, a few weeks had sufficed to bring home a considerable number of the cruisers, and, fortunately, Commodore Stringham found himself in harmony with the army commander at Fortress Monroe. Some correspondence relative to the contemplated attack on Hatteras Inlet had taken place with the War Department, but it steadfastly refused to assume any responsibility, except to furnish such troops as were required for landing and assisting the navy in the attack. It was even specified in the orders that the troops thus detailed should return to Hampton Roads as soon as the object of the expedition was attained.

Perhaps a little digression is justifiable here to say a word about Gen. Benjamin F. Butler, who was in immediate command of the forces. I say in immediate command, for his nominal superior was one of the superannuated officers of the old army to whom I have just referred. However justly General Butler may have laid himself open to criticism by some of his subsequent military and other operations, he was at this time deserving of high praise for certain bold and independent actions that had won brilliant success and brought his name prominently before the country.

It was perhaps excusable, therefore, for a sailor boy to take a short shore leave while the Hatteras expedition is in preparation, and see what was happening, as it were, under the very guns of the fleet. I have already told how General Butler suddenly appeared before dawn on a suspicious-looking steamer off the naval academy at Annapolis. His march to Washington, in company with the New York Seventh Regiment, has also been referred to.

After his arrival at the Capitol, Butler was assigned to the command of the District of Annapolis, which included Baltimore. This city, after its hostile reception of the Massachusetts troops, had been regarded by the authorities at Washington as an almost impregnable stronghold of secession, at least as regards the doubtful State of Maryland. The governor of the State was inclined to be faithful to the Union, but even he was afraid that if any stringent measures were undertaken in Baltimore the city would rise in revolt, and the State would be precipitated into participation in the Rebellion.

Butler fixed his headquarters at the Relay House, midway between Annapolis and Washington, and very soon satisfied himself that nothing stood in the way of his marching in any direction that pleased him best. He communicated his ideas to the major-general in command, and was told loftily that the subject was under consideration and that as soon as a force of twelve thousand men could be spared from the defenses of the Capitol an attempt would probably be made to occupy Baltimore.

General Butler was nothing if not independent, so, without asking leave of anybody, he started with his regiment on the night of May thirteenth, and in the darkness of the early morning hours of the next day marched into Baltimore without opposition, seized Fort Federal Hill, commanding the city and harbor, fortified himself there without any opposition whatever, and notified the municipal authorities that he had come to stay, and that United States troops would thereafter be guaranteed safe passage through the city.

While on his way to Baltimore the same night he detached a company of his regiment to go to Frederick, Maryland, and arrest a prominent secessionist who had been making more trouble for the United States Government than any one else in the State, furnishing arms, subscribing funds to equip companies of Confederate soldiers, and, in short, doing all that he could to force the State into alliance with the Confederacy. This gentleman was summarily carried to Baltimore and placed under guard in Butler's headquarters, only to be released within a few hours by order of the Secretary of State.

The idea of two such successful expeditions carried out without authority and with a ridiculously inadequate force was too much for the equanimity of the good old major-general commanding. As soon as he heard the news he wrote to General Butler:—

" Sir, your hazardous occupation of Baltimore was undertaken without my knowledge, and, of course, without my approbation . . . It is also reported that you have sent a detachment to Frederick, but that is impossible."

The old general could not calmly surrender the idea of occupying Baltimore according to his ideas of military etiquette with a force of, at least, twelve thousand men; that a little Yankee general should have accomplished this with a single regiment, and at the same time have effected what was regarded as " impossible " with one, and no more than one company of infantry, could not be reconciled with any due respect for the regulations of the army of the United States.

The president and cabinet, however, not having as yet been impressed by the necessity of doing things strictly according to rule, immediately held a meeting and promoted Butler to be a major-general of volunteers, the senior of that grade in the service.

As he continued to assert that he could hold Baltimore as easily as he "could hold his own hat," and that "a yellow dog was sufficient escort for him in any part of Maryland," he was evidently unfit to remain in command. Therefore, he was relieved of duty in Baltimore, and sent to Fortress Monroe, where it was thought he could not, for a time, at least, do any especial harm. As a precautionary measure, however, the other old officer to whom reference has been made was placed in command over him.

But the Yankee general was not to be repressed. The first thing that he discovered was that the garrison at Fortress Monroe was supplied with water from a distant source and brought within the gates by the primitive method of a mule team. His representation of this state of things threatened to strain his relations still further with the War Department, which had always been taught to regard this means of supply as adequate for the small garrison maintained in time of peace.

His next escapade was perpetrated on the twenty-fourth of May, and was the invention of a phrase that has since almost immortalized him;

namely, the term "contraband" as applied to escaped negro slaves seeking refuge within our lines. Three such negroes, belonging to a certain Colonel Mallory of the Confederate Army, had been employed on the fortifications at Sewell's Point, and, learning that their master intended to transport his entire domestic establishment from Virginia to Florida for their greater security, these three enterprising chattels made up their minds to desert.

Whether they begged, borrowed, or stole the boat in which they effected their escape is not known, but certain it is that on the morning in question they were descried making their way across the channel from the rebel battery. How they managed to make their escape without being fired upon has never been explained. Butler promptly put them to work, and soon afterwards was notified that a flag of truce was approaching his picket line a short distance inland.

Sending word by the messenger that he would immediately repair to the rendezvous, he rode thither, and met Major Carey, of Virginia, with whom he had a previous acquaintance, having met him at the Charleston convention, just before the last presidential campaign. The situation must have been rather odd for both these men, meeting one day as members of the Democratic National Convention, and the next, riding up to meet one another on a hostile picket line; one claiming allegiance to a far Southern State now seceded from the Union, and seeking to overthrow the government which it had helped to establish; the other harboring fugitive slaves in the name of the United States.

After some conversation on matters relating to the safe conduct of white fugitives who wished to seek a haven of safety in the North, the major propounded the subject of the three slaves. "What are you going to do with them?" he asked.

"I intend to hold them," said Butler.

"The Constitution of the United States requires you to return them to their owner," said the major.

"Virginia passed an ordinance of secession the other day. I am under no such obligations to a foreign country," said Butler.

"But," replied the major, "you say that we cannot secede."

"But you say that you have seceded. I shall hold these negroes as 'contraband of war;' since they were engaged in the construction of your battery. The simple question is, shall they be used for or against the United States? And, unless I receive contrary orders from the Secretary of War, I shall give the United States the benefit of the doubt.*

The consternation of the Cabinet at Washington may be imagined when this new and original interpretation of constitutional and international law was brought before them. High legal authorities all over the land declared for or against General Butler's position, according to personal belief, but the comical side of his decision captivated the public at large. The comic papers published cartoons, and the funny columns of the daily papers exhausted the subject in epigrams. The witty and impromptu decision of this Yankee soldier lawyer carried the nation with it, and neither the Secretary of State nor the Secretary of War ventured to countermand Butler's orders. The phrase was so apt that escaped slaves remained " contrabands " until they became " freedmen."

---

* This account is slightly condensed from General Butler's own narrative of the interview.

CHAPTER X.

COMMODORE STRINGHAM and General Butler took kindly to one another from the first, and cooperated cordially whenever possible. Butler knew pretty well how to manage his immediate superior, who was very well satisfied to remain in his quarters, as long as some one else would originate ideas and take the responsibility of their execution.

Practically the details of the expedition, so far as concerned the land forces, were left in Butler's hands. He engaged transports and, in harmony with the plans of the commodore, about one thousand men were embarked with rations for ten days, and the entire fleet sailed on the twenty-sixth of August. Leaving Hampton Roads early in the day, they rounded Cape Hatteras, which, fortunately, belied its stormy character in their behalf, and came to anchor without accident the same afternoon near the inlet.

The two big sister frigates, "Minnesota" and

" Wabash," led the line, and quite a fleet of gun-boats and transports, including the little " Otter," trailed out astern of them. One or two old-fashioned sailing frigates had started out in advance of the fleet, and were, of course, distanced by the steamers.

The situation at Hatteras Inlet can only be understood by reference to the map. From the inlet to Cape Hatteras is a stretch of twelve miles of desolate beach, on which it was intended the troops should land, well beyond range of the guns of the forts. The process of landing was begun as soon as the fleet arrived, as the sea was quite calm, and the fickleness of the Hatteras weather is well known to all sea-going folk.

The army had come provided with a clumsy species of surf boat, especially constructed for the purpose and rather ill adapted to carrying it out. With the assistance of some of the navy boats, however, some three or four hundred men were landed, with two effective boat howitzers and the necessary supply of ammunition. Several of the boats were upset in the surf, and as evening drew on most of them were swamped or disabled. At this time, too, the weather became threatening and the flagship signaled that the whole squadron should draw off shore.

Commodore Stringham would certainly never have given this signal from his flagship had he known that it was destined to involve a modest sailor boy of the " Otter " in his first case of absence without leave.

My boat's crew had been one of those detailed to go ashore and assist in landing the troops. To accomplish this our boat had been beached during the quiet hours of the afternoon, and, as I was nothing but a boy and was not expected to take part in the heavy work of pulling and hauling, I wandered up to the ridge of the beach and fraternized with the artillery men, who were throwing up temporary breastworks of sand to protect against any attack from the sound or from the direction of the forts. Becoming interested in these operations and in the maneuvers of the small fleet of rebel gunboats now plainly within sight, I had not paid much attention to what was going on upon the outer beach.

My consternation may be imagined, therefore, when, at last, casting a glance in that direction, I saw the " Otter's " boat rising over the outer breakers, some hundred yards from shore. My absence had evidently been overlooked, and here I was destined to pass the night on shore, and, what was worse, supperless, because no rations had been landed with the troops. Most of them, however, had some scraps left over in their haversacks, and were disposed to be generous to a sailor boy, so that we were not entirely without means of subsistence.

The captain of the company, with whose men I had made friends, told me that, under the circumstances, I had better report to Colonel Webber, of the Twentieth New York Volunteers, who had landed, and was in command of the detachment. He was standing by a fire of driftwood, trying to dry himself after a ducking incurred during the process of landing, and laughed when he saw my woe-begone countenance. He told me not to mind, and to make myself as comfortable as I could with Captain Black's company.

There was plenty of driftwood along the beach, and no reason existed why we should not light fires along the seaward slope. The position was easily defended against surprise, for the beach was so narrow that pickets could easily patrol it above and below the bivouac, and we knew that the water of the sound was too shallow for the rebel fleet to approach within effective range. Most of us were pretty thoroughly wet, and were glad enough to try alternately to dry first one side and then the other. I turned in with Captain Black's

company, as it so happened, pretty near the dividing ridge, where the seaward slope changed to that
of the sound.

The night would have passed without any excitement, whatever, but for the negro cook of the
company. He, after the manner of his race, had
started on an exploring expedition sometime during
the small hours. Passing over the beach crest, he
had gone down to the water's edge of the inner
beach, and, finding the sand still warm with the
rays of the August sun, had lain down for an
hour of peaceful contemplation.

He declared solemnly that he did not go to sleep,
but that he was, in fact, "laying low," with his
eyes near the level of the water, so that he could
the better observe certain suspicious movements
which he thought he detected on the part of the
hostile fleet.

At any rate, he was suddenly startled by per-
ceiving what he took to be two rebel gunboats in
the nature of ironclads emerging from the water
and approaching his resting-place. Naturally he
sprang up, and, with a shriek of terror, fled toward
the bivouac. As ill luck would have it, he cleared
the ridge just where I and my companions were
lying, and, stumbling over us, fell headlong upon
the men next beyond us. Of course, there was an

instant alarm : the gunners jumped to their stations,
men seized their rifles, and it would have taken
little more to set everybody to shooting at anything
that moved.

The captain's voice, however, restrained the
panic, which he soon learned had been caused by
the black cook. This individual, upon being
questioned, related his terrible experience upon the
beach, and assured the captain that two rebel ironclads were coming ashore to annihilate the entire
command. The captain, of course, thought that
the fellow had been frightened by some chance
prowler, but decided that he would look over the
ridge and see for himself. Half a dozen men
accompanied him, including myself, of course,
and as we looked down upon the beach level there
certainly was something extraordinary going on
near the water's edge. We could hear muffled
sounds as of blows and scrapings, but what it all
meant no one had the slightest idea.

Ordering a cautious advance, the captain led the
way down the slope, revolver in hand, and I must
confess that his followers were not over anxious to
keep pace with him, for there was something very
uncanny about the appearance of this shapeless
but moving mass. At length the captain halted,
put up his hand to shade his eyes from the light of

the stars, and after a moment's inspection broke into a quiet laugh.

" Come on, boys," he said ; " we'll have something for breakfast after all. It's a pair of sea-turtles come ashore to fight. They do that at this season. I've been down this coast before, and have caught them many a time. Where is that black rascal of a cook ? "

Jim had prudently remained behind, but was quickly hauled from his hiding-place, and made to join in the skirmish line that surrounded the struggling turtles and turned them over on their backs. He was still under the spell of terror, and in his eyes they seemed gigantic monsters ready to work his destruction. He was compelled, however, to assist in the capture, and was straightway set to work cutting up the prisoners, and preparing them for the morning meal. By the time this was done there were faint indications of daylight in the east, and, although we had no coffee to help out our repast, turtle soup and turtle steak for breakfast were not so bad when we could get nothing else.

The sea had gone down by morning, so that more of the soldiers could be landed on the beach without difficulty, and I managed to get myself taken off at an early hour by one of the Monticello's boats, whose coxswain was kind enough to put me on board my own ship. I found that my absence had not been discovered until after dark, when it was impracticable to send ashore for me, supposing I was safe with the troops already there.

Practically, of course, this was absence without leave, and I was liable, under ordinary circumstances, to some kind of punishment. My character was fairly good, however, and the division officer only gave me a moderate blowing-up for heedlessness in letting the boat get away. Indeed, I think the coxswain of the boat got a worse wigging than I did, because he had failed to notice my absence.

There was no special need of haste in beginning offensive operations, so the commodore took his own time about it. The forts on the end of the sand spit were quite isolated from the mainland; no reenforcements could reach them from the sound without coming inside the range of our rifled guns, and any reenforcements landed on the beach could easily be dispersed, if not by the troops, then by the fire of the fleet. The commodore, therefore, allowed all his command to have a comfortable breakfast before ordering his ships to take up their stations and open fire.

GETTING INTO ACTION OFF HATTERAS.

There were two forts at the inlet, namely, Fort Hatteras and Fort Clark ; the first named, and more important of the works, being close to the inlet proper, while the other was farther out toward the ocean, situated on a low point, and separated from the larger earthworks by a shallow lagoon. The fleet anchored so that the two forts were nearly in a line with one another, and shot passing over one might possibly fall upon the other.

The superiority of the artillery of the fleet was quickly obvious. Fort Clark was soon silenced ; the men deserting their guns and wading across the shallow lagoon that separated them from the shelter of the larger fort. Upon this the troops advanced along the beach, and by two o'clock in the afternoon the national ensign was floating over the ramparts.

It was supposed at this time that Fort Hatteras, too, had been abandoned, as its fire had altogether ceased and no flag was displayed upon its flagstaff. Accordingly, the " Monticello " was directed to attempt the passage of the inlet, but no sooner was she well within the breakers than the cannonade was resumed, and for a few minutes she was in imminent danger of being sunk. Upon this the flagship, with the " Susquehanna " and " Pawnee," which were opposite the fort, resumed their fire which continued until sunset, when the fleet drew off for the night.

Next morning the bombardment was resumed, vessels anchoring directly off the inlet and sending heavy projectiles from their long pivot guns into the forts that still held out. It was a one-sided affair, — this capture of the forts at Hatteras,— mere target practise so far as any danger to the fleet was concerned.

Superior artillery enabled it to remain safely beyond the range of rebel guns, and it was soon apparent that the fort was too hot a place for further defense. Shortly before noon a large shell penetrated one of the ventilators of the magazine, and so narrowly missed blowing the whole establishment to pieces that a white flag was raised preliminary to surrender.

The army tug, "Fanny," with General Butler on board, had been close at hand, watching proceedings, and with characteristic promptness the general ordered her at once within the inlet. Beyond the bulkhead were two or three Confederate vessels, including one laden with troops, and the general gave them a rifle shot from his six-inch pivot gun that went well over toward the rebel gunboats, which had not yet given any indication of surrender, and were dangerously near at hand.

They speedily took the hint and made for safer quarters.

Upon this General Butler sent a boat with an officer, asking the meaning of the white flag, and presently received a conditional offer of surrender, which he declined, sending word back that the surrender must be unconditional. After some slight delay, word was returned accepting these terms, and shortly afterward the commanding officer of the fort, with some of his staff, came on board the "Fanny."

This gentleman was Captain Samuel Barron, C. S. N., late of the United States Navy, and some of his officers had only a few weeks before held the commission of the United States. It is not altogether easy to conceive the frame of mind with which these proud secessionists went on board the commodore's flagship, where many of the officers had formerly been their shipmates and whom they had no doubt treated with the supercilious arrogance that was too common among Southerners about to resign their allegiance. More than one of them must have asked himself while awaiting the conclusion of the negotiations what the Southern secession leaders could have meant in persuading their followers to believe that the Yankees would never fight.

But while these negotiations were going on the situation had become somewhat critical under the guns of the fort. The "Monticello" in attempting to pass over the bar, had grounded within easy range, and the "Adelaide," an army transport, crowded with troops, had followed her example. It is not at all beyond the range of possibility that if this had occurred before Captain Barron left the fort he would have succeeded in obtaining better terms for surrender.

The game was lost, however; the articles of capitulation were signed; more than seven hundred men surrendered as prisoners of war, with a thousand stand of arms, thirty cannon, five stand of colors, a brig loaded with cotton, and sundry stores of provisions, including one hundred and fifty bags of coffee. But far exceeding all these was the strategic value of the position that fell into our hands. In effect, the whole wide extent of the Carolina Sound was under the control of our guns, which would otherwise have afforded a safe refuge for privateers, cruisers, and blockade runners.

The Hatteras expedition was in reality the first noteworthy success of the Union arms on land or sea, and, coming soon after the disastrous defeat of the army at Bull Run, went far to encourage the Government in its measures to organize an ener-

getic campaign. Owing to the superiority of our
armament, the affair assumed, after all, a certain
holiday aspect, for not a single man was hurt on
the national side. Several were killed and wounded
in the fort, but their exact number was never
known.

Here again General Butler's readiness to disobey
orders stood him and the country in good stead.
On looking over the situation, he saw at a glance
the importance of maintaining a permanent garrison
at this point, and on consultation with Commodore
Stringham he decided to leave enough men to hold
the position against any possible rebel attack. His
orders were to return at once to Fortress Monroe
with his entire detachment, but he knew perfectly
well that if he allowed the Department to receive
his report through the regular channels and learn
how its directions had been ignored he would be
reprimanded, if not court-marshalled, for disobe-
dience of orders.

Accordingly, while Commodore Stringham took
the prisoners on board his flagship and sailed for
New York, General Butler embarked in his despatch boat, the " Fanny," and made the best possible time direct to Washington. Arriving there
in the middle of the night, he aroused one of the
cabinet officers, and together they went to the White

House and imparted their good news to the president. Lincoln was overjoyed at this, the first substantial success of the national arms, and before the War Department had fairly waked up the next morning a cabinet meeting had been called, and it was voted that the army should continue to hold Hatteras Inlet, with such aid from the navy as was deemed necessary.

CHAPTER XI.

CONTRABANDS AS COAST PILOTS.

NO sooner had the Rebels lost control of Pamlico Sound and its tributaries than they made energetic efforts to keep control of the adjacent waters to the northward. Roanoke Island afforded the key to this position, and now that Pamlico Sound was practically under the control of the navy its reduction was probably only a question of time.

The blockade, as yet, was not effectual. A few vessels were stationed off Charleston, Savannah, and a few of the more important ports of entry, but when it is remembered that the whole Southern coast is a series of river mouths, harbors, and estuaries, all more or less navigable to vessels of considerable size, the wonder is that any sort of a blockade was maintained. The fact remains, however, that, although the rebels did all in their power to convince their British friends of its inefficiency, they never succeeded.

A British gunboat, the " Gladiator," cruised at

least twice up and down the Atlantic coast to ascertain the true state of affairs. Captain Hinck-
ley made his report, presumably adverse to the
national cause, but in the meantime several hundred foreign vessels, including numerous British
blockade runners, had been captured by our
vessels, taken into the nearest ports, condemned
by admiralty courts and, except in a very few
cases, no protests were made. In short, after it
was once fairly in working order, the maritime
nations of the world reluctantly confessed that the
blockade was effectual enough to be recognized,
or, at least, too effectual to be ignored.

The station in Hampton Roads was pleasant
enough as navy life goes, and not without its
temporary excitement. The intelligent contraband
brought rumors from every direction of marching
troops and of gunboats and ironclads that were
being rapidly prepared at the Norfolk Navy Yard.
The "Merrimac" had been raised and was covered
with iron plates, and at Richmond other swift
rams were in course of preparation. These
rumors and announcements were somewhat pre-
mature, although, as we afterwards learned, they
were not altogether false.

According to the regulations of Uncle Sam's
navy, the boys on board ship are required to de-

vote certain hours to study. Sailor boys are not
any more fond of study than their shore-going
brethren; still, the rule was reasonably well enforced; but it was presently discovered by the
teachers who were detailed to take charge of us
that I had advanced far beyond all that could
possibly be required of a powder monkey.

Therefore, it came to pass when it was found
that I could write a fairly good schoolboy hand,
and was reasonably trustworthy at copying, that I
was promoted to a kind of clerkship which, while
it did not interfere with other duties to any serious
extent, gave me privileges that were not unac-
ceptable. It brought me into relations with the
best of the wardroom officers and made it possible
for me to go on various expeditions from which I
would otherwise have been excluded.

Occasionally the " Otter " was sent on some
minor expedition, but our ordinary life on board
would have been unspeakably dull but for the fact
that everybody had his regular work. This is the
grand secret of all discipline. If idleness were
permitted on board a man-of-war, with its hun-
dreds of men in close quarters, there would be
mutiny within a week. Upon the whole, therefore, it was acceptable when it began to be whispered about that the " Otter " was again under

orders. How such news gains currency nobody knows. It seems to be in the air, and when the order comes to take on a full supply of coal and stores for a voyage nobody is taken very much by surprise.

We were ready in a day or two, and an extra force of volunteers was called for from the New England regiments. A hundred men responded, mainly from Marblehead, Gloucester, Newburyport, and the other sea-going headquarters of that rugged coast. It was tolerably evident, therefore, that some sort of hazardous work was expected of us. The volunteer sailor men came aboard with their blankets, knapsacks, and rifles, and were stowed away wherever there was room for them to lie on deck. Nearly all were sailor men, and many were the jokes perpetrated about going to sea with rifles and knapsacks. Naturally, they fraternized fairly well with our own crew, who forthwith dubbed them "the horse marines," a nickname by which they were known to the end of the expedition, and which they accepted with very good grace.

We got under way on October 2, and on the following day rounded to off a low-lying cape partly covered with a growth of cypress or pine, and marked by an abandoned lighthouse, whose light had been extinguished by the Confederacy. This was the mouth of Winyah Bay, at the head of which was situated Georgetown, S. C., about twelve miles from the sea.

Coming to anchor outside the breakers, boats were sent to sound out the channel and see if any sunken obstruction existed. Everything was clear, and the little "Otter" was soon anchored in five fathoms of water opposite the lighthouse and behind the shelter of the sand spit on which it stood. On the opposite side of the bay was a straggling hamlet, where we could see quite an unheard-of commotion among the inhabitants at our unwelcome appearance.

The lighthouse being close at hand, it was necessary first to make sure that there were no fortifications or troops in its vicinity. An officer was accordingly sent to investigate, and found the light-keeper still in possession of his quarters and rather disposed than otherwise to be civil in his replies. There was absolutely no indication of military occupation about the point nor in the woods which made out within a few hundred yards of the government reservation; the keeper assured us, in fact, that nothing had been done toward fortifying the point.

Toward the latter part of the afternoon a small

steamer came down from Georgetown and took a
look at us, but, not seeing anything to invite a
closer acquaintance, returned whence she came.
It was, therefore, certain that news of our arrival
had reached the mainland, and the nearest military
authorities were no doubt advised of our presence.

It was a rather dark, starlight night, and after
the glow had quite faded from the west two armed
boats were despatched under charge of Lieutenant
Casey, who had long since returned with his prize
crew, on a pilot-hunting expedition. Guessing
that the hamlet, which has already been referred
to, was mainly composed of fishermen's huts and
possibly of pilot's houses, Captain Ross had
directed us to go ashore and see what we could
effect. Some caution was necessary, for the malig-
nity and desperate hatred of Yankees that was
cherished by all Southern communities at that time
is difficult of belief now that it is all over.

We pulled in the direction of the hamlet with
perfect silence, the oars being carefully muffled, and
presently drew near enough to perceive a few dim
lights in the windows and to hear occasional voices
along the shore. Under the supervision of Captain
Ross, each of the boats had been provided with
certain fireworks designed to assist our enterprise.
The lower part of some casks had been sawn off

and filled with a mixture of oakum soaked with melted pitch and turpentine; there were four of these altogether, and one of them was provided, in addition to the slow match common to all, with a rocket and a Roman candle.

The boats paused a short distance off shore, and the slow match that was attached to the rocket was lighted, the tub put softly overboard into the water, an anchor line dropped after it, and then we shoved off, leaving it to its fate. The boats pulled away some two hundred yards and then lay side by side, end on toward the town, with black tarpaulins hung over the bows so as to conceal the white paint from observers on shore. The match was timed " long " for ten minutes, and at the end of about twelve the rocket went whizzing aloft; the Roman candle followed, sending its brilliant balls high up into the air, and then, as it in turn died down, the quick match connecting with the flare caught fire, and there was straightway a bright blaze rising apparently from the surface of the sea, and lighting the beach for an eighth of a mile in both directions.

Hardly had the boom of the rocket bursting on high died away when cries of all sorts arose in the little settlement, — cries of wonder and admiration and some few of fear. Doors opened, lights shone out, and the whole population stood spell-bound as the brilliant balls from the Roman candle soared successively aloft. Then followed the steady blaze of the oakum flare, and Casey looked the ground over with his glasses. Not a sign of military organization was visible anywhere, and there were not more than a half a dozen white men in sight, all told.

One of the better-looking houses had a flagstaff in front of it, which might possibly be intended for a signal station. It was not within reason that there could be any formidable armed force in the place, for, whether such a force had been com-posed of raw levies or of seasoned veterans, it would certainly have sprung to its arms, and there was no indication of any such movement. While the people on shore were rubbing their eyes and trying to peer into the surrounding darkness, Casey stood up and hailed : —

"Hallo, on shore there, we won't fire unless you do, so don't be frightened. But if you do fire on us we'll burn down the whole place, so be careful. Now, I am coming ashore. Take oars! Give way all!"

We were but a short distance from the beach, so that hardly more than two minutes had elapsed before the bows grated on the sand, and the crew

of our boat sprang smartly ashore in front of the
flagstaff. By Casey's orders, the other crew remained afloat ready to shove off at a moment's
notice. Our crew deployed smartly with ready
cocked carbines "at the carry." Another of the
prepared flares was lighted on the beach as Casey
walked forward.

The landing had been effected immediately in
front of the best quarter of the settlement, the
quarter, that is, where the white people were
gathered, and to them Casey addressed himself.

"I suppose you are all South Carolinians and
Secessionists," he said. "We are from the Federal gunboat out there in the stream, and we're
going to stay here as long as it suits us. Understand, once for all, that we don't intend to do you
any harm unless we're attacked, but if you make
any trouble, or let anybody fire on us from the
shore, we'll burn the entire outfit.

The whole population, white and colored, had
turned out, as curiosity overcame fear, and quite a
crowd had pressed forward to the vicinity of the
fire. Casey waved them back. "Don't come
any nearer," he said, "till I call you."

Three rather ruffianly white men stood about
the door of the principal house, and a few others
near them, while a few slatternly looking women

peered from the doors of the neighboring houses.
Casey looked round over the crowd of sable
visages in the firelight, and, selecting a venerable
old darky, probably attracted to him by the whiteness of his wool, he sung out: "Here, Uncle!
You come here." The old man shambled forward, a tall, stooping figure, with a dilapidated
straw hat in his hand, glancing deprecatingly
at the burly white man as if asking permission to
come forward.

"What's your name, uncle?"

"Bob, sah."

"Bob what?"

"Bob Randall, sah."

"How old are you?"

"Don't know, marsa; mos' one hundred years,
I 'spec'."

"Who do you belong to?"

"Marsa Jim Randall, sah."

"Where is he?"

"He ober to the big house, ober on Santee."

"What are you here for, Bob?"

At this the more important-looking of the white
men interposed. "Here, mister, he's my nigger;
ask your questions of me, if you want to." The
man came forward as he spoke.

"I'll talk to you presently," said Casey sharply.

" Meanwhile, step back and keep still." Then in
a lower voice : " Now, Bob, do you like to stay
here? "

" Not over muchly, marsa," glancing apprehensively over his shoulder.

" Like to go back to the old house sometimes,
don't you? "

" Oh, yes, marsa."

" Folks there? "

" Yes, sah."

" Well, now, Bob, if you'll come with me I'll
give you a chance to go back to the big house and
see your folks, and I want you to bring two good
coast pilots with you,— boys that know both the
Santees, and Bull's Bay, and all the rest down
below Cape Romain to Charleston. You needn't
be afraid of him," nodding toward the white man,
who looked on with a scowl. " Now, you go and
get two good boys. They shall have good pay
and food."

Bob shambled away, and the big white man
started to follow him.

" Stop where you are," cried Casey. " Boys,
keep those men covered with your carbines.
Come ashore, second cutter."

Reenforced by the second crew, the whites
abandoned whatever ideas of escape or resistance

they may have entertained, and suffered themselves to be searched and disarmed. For, after
the manner of the South Carolinian of the period,
the three carried heavy revolvers in their belts.

"Sorry, Mr. ——, excuse me, I don't know
your name. But under the circumstances I shall
have to search the house. Bring a lantern, quarter-
master."

Brown brought a lantern from the boat, and the
two with ready revolvers proceeded to search the
house. Nothing of a suspicious character was
found beyond a rather liberal supply of firearms
and provisions, which seemed excessive and unnecessary to Northern eyes.

"I'll leave you a good shotgun," Casey said,
"for I know you depend largely on game for a
living hereabouts, but I must take the rest of these
arms on board for safekeeping."

The houses of the other whites were searched,
and a number of other weapons seized. Before
this search was concluded Bob and his two "boys"
were waiting by the boats. Two stalwart, black
fellows in disreputable rags, but both having a
certain air of the seaman about them, and both ex-
pressing themselves ready and willing to act as
pilots for a United States gunboat.

All hands reembarked, and the second cutter

shoved off. The men of the first cutter were in
their places, and Casey was preparing to step
aboard when Bob's master again spoke: " I say,
mister, are you a United States' officer? "

" Yes."

" By what right do you take away my niggers? "

" By the same right that you Southerners took
Fort Sumter the other day."

" Well, you can't take my niggers; I know the
laws of the United States and of South Carolina,
and you can't do it."

" I shall do it, all the same. The United States
requires their services. Evidently you haven't
heard down here that niggers are ' contraband of
war.' Good evening, Mr. ——. By the way,
what is your name? "

The answer to this was something inaudible that
sounded like Jackson, so Casey replied cheerfully,
" Well, good-night, Mr. Jackson; come aboard if
you like; the captain will be glad to see you.
No shooting, though, remember, unless you're
prepared to keep up a pretty lively fight."

The fire on the beach still gave light enough
for us to see the forlorn population gazing after us
as we disappeared in the darkness, and in a few
minutes we heard the hail of the "Otter's" lookout,

rounded to alongside, hoisted the boats aboard, and were once more in the comfortable, well-ordered quarters of our ship. The black pilots were duly presented to the captain, and stood the cross-examination through which he put them very well. They seemed to know all about the vicinity, as negro slaves did in those times, and even old Uncle Bob, who had been the best pilot on the coast in his day, contributed much valuable information in regard to the lay of the land and the various channels available for boat service.

Next morning we got under way, and, after standing out across the bar to explore the different channels of entrance, ran up toward Georgetown, and as soon as we came in sight of its houses bells began to ring and drums beat in expectation of an attack. Our purpose, however, was merely to notify the port authorities that the blockade had been established, a proceeding that is always customary under such circumstances. A warning similar to that given to our acquaintances of the night before was also sent to the military authorities.

Hot-headed Southern officers often got into trouble by opening fire on Government gunboats out of mere bravado, and many a Southern roof-tree was burned because some desperado could not refrain from taking a "pot-shot" at passing Yankees, when no good to their side could possibly result, beyond the killing of one or two men.   Fortunately, there were enough cool heads in Georgetown to restrain local patriotism within the bounds of prudence, and after delivering our messages we steamed back to the anchorage without molestation.

This little excursion up Georgetown Bay was merely a diversion.   Our real purpose was a raid into the Santee country, which was rich in cotton, and therefore tempting to blockade runners. ·

Georgetown, however, after thinking it over, decided that their first reception of us had been somewhat pusillanimous, and, having been reenforced by sundry companies of home guards from the interior, made preparations to annihilate us. These consisted mainly of fire rafts, torpedoes, etc., which generally ran aground before they reached us or refused to explode under any circumstances.

Upon the whole, they afforded us rather more amusement than cause for anxiety, and probably served to keep the volunteers from aggressions that would have caused bloodshed. By daylight we did not habitually have any intercourse with "Pilot Town," but every night one or more of our negro pilots went ashore in a canoe that they had brought with them, visited their friends in the settlement, and kept themselves informed of the various plots that were in preparation.

There were, it appeared, several schooners and sloops loading with cotton in the two Santees and at Georgetown. In the river three of these vessels were reported ready for sea, and Captain Ross determined, if possible, either to destroy or cut them out before they could escape. These three were in the South Santee River, below Brown's Island, and anchored at short intervals, so that one could not well be captured without giving warning to the others. Report had it, moreover, that all of them were provided with armed guards.

The white men who figured in our first visit to the shore had disappeared before " sun-up," as the local phrase has it, the next morning, and not till the next day after that did Uncle Bob, in a chance conversation with the captain and Lieutenant Casey, speak of their leader by name.

" Who did you say? " asked Ross sharply.

" Marsa Jay Hawkson, sah."

Ross and Casey stared at one another aghast.

" Why didn't you tell us that before? "

" Nobody axed me, sah," said Uncle Bob, unconsciously quoting the classic song.

" Did you ask his name, Casey? "

" Yes, sir, and I understood him to say Jackson, or some such name," and Casey's handsome face became very blank. It was evident that he had carelessly missed a chance that was not likely to offer again.

The captain could hardly disguise his vexation.

" Great Scott!" he exclaimed, " what a chance you have lost! The very fellow we are after! Well, never mind, Casey," he added, seeing that officer's chagrin ; " maybe we can give you another chance at him," — prophetic words that were sadly remembered a few days later.

On reviewing the incidents of the first night's expedition, it was evident how the mistake had occurred. Uncle Bob, knowing the man's true name, had understood it correctly when it was given in reply to Casey's inquiry, and supposed that Casey had understood also. The vexatious part was that this Jay Hawkson, a slave trader, was the notorious leader of a local band of Regulators who had hanged two Union men in Georgia a few weeks before. News of this outrage had reached Fortress Monroe, and, hearing that Hawkson was in the Santee country, his capture was planned as part of the " Otter's " duty.

Poor Casey could not forgive himself for having failed to detect and arrest this desperado when he had him within his grasp. Bob declared that he and the boys would find out precisely where he was quartered on the Santee. Indeed, they thought they already knew. It had not occurred to these simple-minded fellows that it was worth while to mention such a commonplace affair as the hanging of one or two Union men and a casual negro or so.

While these things were transpiring, although only two or three days had elapsed, Uncle Bob was pining for the fulfilment of the promise that he should go over to Santee and see the old folks again, and at last Captain Ross consented to let him go ashore and make his way across country, as he could by the devious ways known to the negro slave, so that he could see once more the old cabin that he called home.

The old fellow was a sort of "Uncle Remus," although this latter character was at that time unknown to fiction, and he had become quite a favorite with all hands on board. So, with the promise to return within three days, he was set ashore one evening, and went off in high spirits, thanking everybody for their kindness to the "poor old nigger." That same night, however, a little before daylight, the officer on watch heard something of a rumpus on shore — dogs barking, and shouting that lasted for a little time.   But, as the population of Pilot Town was given to orgies by night when-ever whisky could be obtained in sufficient quan-tities to justify the exertion, he had thought no more of it, and the hours waxed on in quiet.

But as the sun came up and dissipated the thin mists that floated along the river in early morn-ing, ·he made his customary survey of the sur-roundings with a powerful marine glass.   As he swept the shore line in careful inspection, he came to a sudden stop with his glass leveled at the town. Something was hanging on the limb of one of the trees, something unfamiliar, something that hung heavily down and yet swayed and twisted in ghastly fashion in the gentle morning breeze.   A boat was at once lowered and sent to investigate.   Sure enough, it was poor old Uncle Bob, who had been waylaid by the Regulators, brought back to the scene of his servitude, and hanged defiantly, under cover of darkness, within easy range of his pro-tectors' guns.

The remaining negro population of Pilot Town was in terrified retirement, Hawkson and his gang having been liberal with blows and threats.   But as the rising sun warmed their bodies and vanished their fears to some extent, they came out of their hiding-places and told the story.   The regulators

had been recognized as they performed their act
of vengeance, and had promptly ridden away before the light of dawn appeared in the East, leaving behind them threats of dire vengeance should
any further aid be given to the Yankee invaders.

Of course this atrocious act made us all the more
anxious to carry out the purpose of our expedition,
and many were the vows of vengeance registered
that day on board the " Otter " as the venerable old
slave was buried in the sand with the honors of
war, Captain Ross reading the burial service, and
the ragged negro population standing around with
faces still ashy from fright.

CHAPTER XII.

THE SLAVE DRIVER OF SANTEE.

THE shore expeditions of our negro pilots were rendered still more hazardous by this experience. Nevertheless, they were brave enough, and did not hesitate to venture ashore when their friends signaled that the coast was clear. As soon as it was definitely learned where Hawkson's headquarters were, preparations began for as formidable an expedition as could be managed with the "Otter's" resources. With a view to some such emergency, and considering our largely increased strength of numbers from the addition of the volunteer "horse marines," we had come provided with extra boats, so that, leaving enough men on board to work the ship, and even defend her in case of need, we could muster one hundred and fifty men for the expedition. Ever since coming into the bay soldiers and sailors had alike been drilled in embarking and landing under various conditions, Lighthouse Point being well adapted for such exercises.

Our pilots were doubtful about getting over the South Santee bar at night, but declared their ability to do so by daylight at any time except dead low tide. One evening, accordingly, after dark, we slipped our cable, and dropped down the channel with all lights housed, and ran round the few miles intervening to the mouth of the Santee. The sea was comparatively calm, and boats were lowered, and the soldiers and sailors boarded them without confusion, their persistent drills having rendered it possible to effect this without confusion, even when the ship was rolling in the seaway.

Our two pilots had both been so anxious to go on this expedition, that they had to be allowed to draw lots in order to prevent them from coming to blows. But at last a decision was reached in favor of black Joe, perhaps the best of the two, although there was, in fact, little to choose between them.

For the benefit of Northern readers, it should, perhaps, be explained that many of the pilots along our Southern coast at that time were negro slaves. Often they were hired out by their owners and employed by white men who lived near the coast and turned an honest penny by pocketing pilot fees for their own benefit.

This had been the case with poor Uncle Bob and the two boys whom he had brought to us. Often the coast pilots were men of high courage and great native intelligence, as was the case notably with Robert Small, who made his escape from Charleston, carrying out a steamer of which he was the pilot, and surrendering her to the blockading fleet in the offing.

Under conduct of our less famous Joe, the boats fell into column, and pulled away from the ship toward the place where the rollers were growling on the shoal water of the bar. Joe stood up in the bow of the leading boat, " nosing out " the deepest water with that extraordinary instinct that belongs to the born pilot, and very soon the five heavily laden boats, after tossing for a few moments somewhat perilously, passed over into the quiet water within the bar. The tide was beginning to run flood, and after half an hour of leisurely rowing, the whole flotilla was well behind the southern point of Cedar Island which separates the two Santees.

It was believed to be about five miles to the place where Hawkson was supposed to have his headquarters,— A plantation house well known to our guide, who had clearly described its surroundings. It was pretty certain that he would have his gang with him, but how many was purely a matter of conjecture. That they were all desperate characters and well armed was certain, and it was more than probable that they would make a resistance worthy their reputation, no matter how large the odds might be that were brought against them.

The three schooners that I have mentioned before as being ready for sea were between the mouth of the river and this ultimate point of our destination, but precisely where we did not know. We had to pass them before reaching our goal, but hoped to effect this undiscovered, by keeping along the south shore of the river, where we could take advantage of the shelter afforded by certain islands and be at the same time at the greatest possible distance from the anchored vessels.

I had managed to smuggle myself into the leading boat, on the plea of carrying Lieutenant Casey's haversack for him, and crouched close behind Pilot Joe as he stood up in the bow. I considered myself about as keen sighted a youngster as any afloat, but black Joe taught me a lesson as to my own inferiority. I soon found that he could see objects on shore and in the water with great distinctness long before I could make them out at all. In short, he had veritable owls' eyes, a gift not uncommon among his race, and peculiarly cultivated, of course, by those in his calling.

This was really my first serious experience of an expedition probably involving an encounter with the enemy and more or less loss of life. The affair of Hatteras, while far more formidable in the eyes of the world and more important in history, was a very different affair from this.

The familiar surroundings of every-day naval life, the consciousness of being supported by ship-mates, by big guns with trained men behind them, all conspired to impart a feeling of confidence, and I had been full of fight from the time when the first shot was fired. It was a very different matter,— this dark and silent river, the low, sullen grumbling of the bar as we left it astern, the cloudy sky overhead, barely touched in spots by the dim light of the young moon, the measured swish of oars, the dark, swaying forms of men.

I could not for the life of me help remembering that River of Death that I had so often heard about in the old church at Stonyhaven, and which I had pretty well forgotten since my enlistment. Before I knew it I was saying over to myself the refrain of a hymn that I had once heard at a camp-meeting : —

> "One dark river to cross,
> One dark river to cross."

Over and over this fateful line insisted on repeating itself, and I was fast getting into what our English cousins call " a blue funk " when Joe whispered, " Dah's one of dem schooners."

My nervousness vanished in an instant, and I strained my eyes into the darkness, but not a suggestion could I see of anything like a schooner. However, I passed the word aft, as in duty bound.

" Avast pulling, men," said Casey, in low tone, and the other boats, following suit, drifted on in absolute silence with the flowing tide.

Casey came forward, stepping lightly from thwart to thwart, and stood with his hand on Joe's shoulder.

" Whereaway is she, Joe? "

" Right ahead, Marsa Casey," and he pointed into the blackness of the pine forest that bordered the shore.

Casey adjusted his night glasses, and after a long, silent look, " Blest if I can see a thing," he said.

" She dah, sure enough, Marsa Casey. I'se got cat's eyes, I has. I kin see her plain. She's got a deckload of cotton bales."

" Well," Casey said, " show us the best way to get past, whether she's there or not."

So the flotilla altered its course and managed to drift by without attracting attention. Indeed, it was not until we were opposite the point that Joe had indicated that we made out a dim light apparently coming from the cabin windows.

Rowing was resumed as soon as a safe distance had been passed, and Joe directed our course behind the islands before referred to, which extended the better part of a mile along the southern shore of the river. As we passed the cut between two of these islands, Joe remarked, "Dah's anuder on 'em, sah," and in due course most of us were able to see a dim tracery of topmasts against the sky.

When we came out into the open water above the island, where the river takes a wide sweep to the southward, the third and last of the three could be seen, or, rather, Joe said that she could be seen, at anchor under the farther shore. They were at such a distance, however, that, with the wind toward us, there was no danger of their hearing the sound of our oars.

About half a mile above the upper island, Joe broke the silence with, "Most dah now, Mars Cap'n," and he said further that the river was clear above. Going aft, he took the helm, and steered our boat into the bank. This place was about a third of a mile below our destination, and, as there was a fairish shore for landing, the boats were pulled up against the bank, and all hands disembarked to recover from the cramped position

of the last three hours. Joe, at his own suggestion, went alone to look over the ground before the
men advanced farther.

"I don't reckon I won't be gone not more'n a
half an hour, Marsa Cap'n," he said, executing
one of the extraordinary triple negatives common
among the Southern negroes and low-down whites;
"not more'n a half an hour, Marsa Cap'n; dar's
a dog I wants to get shut up if I anyways kin."

The path by which Joe disappeared was at once
picketed, three men being stationed in the woods
to guard against surprise. In a few minutes we
heard a fierce barking in the direction of the
plantation, which quickly subsided to a whine of
recognition, and then all became quiet again.
Another long interval, and then the picket chal-
lenge cautiously.

"All right, it's me," was the answer in Joe's
voice.

"Coast all clar, Marsa Casey, but I s'pect de
dogs round de big house is goin' for to make
trouble. I didn't darst to go very nigh. Now
here's de way it am, Marsa Casey. De parf
goes straight along shore through de woods from
here to de aidge of de clearin'. De nigger quarters is on de lef, and de big house on de right, just
afore yer. De nigger dogs is all shet up."

Casey told the men to fall in, the "horse marine" captain forming up his men in good shape. This captain, by the way, was ranking officer, but, like the sensible fellow he was, he had waived rank in view of the semi-naval character of the expedition. In single file, the detachment moved off into the dark path, with some unavoidable clankings of accouterments and occasional stumblings over cypress knees or other obstructions.

It is only savage war parties that can move with absolute silence through an unknown country, especially if it is heavily wooded. There is always something about the equipment of a civilized soldier that rattles or clanks at an unexpected moment. Hence, it is almost out of the question to steal undiscovered upon a vigilant enemy. In the present case we did not count upon the enemy's being vigilant. His most trustworthy videttes, the dogs of the negro quarter, were in confinement, and, barring accidents, we could come well out of the woods before detection from the plantation house, which was our objective point.

On reaching the opening, our guide halted, and the officers had a consultation. The stars gave light enough to see the big house, a low, wide-

roofed structure, with overhanging eaves and ve-
randas surrounding it, in the usual Southern style.
On looking over the ground, the plan of operations
was quickly perfected and explained to the men.
The detachment divided, part going round in the
rear of the house, and the other skirting the river
bank so as to pass in front of it and join the others
when the circuit was completed, while a third detachment, acting as a reserve under Casey himself,
was to wait till the house was nearly surrounded
and then advance directly by the path.

The men stepped off when the word was given
to advance, following one another and taking intervals as they went, each one, that is, allowing his
leader to go five or six paces before following
him.

"Now, Marsa Cap'n," said Joe at this point, "if
you'll scuse dis chile he'll just stay right yere wid
the doctor by dis big gum tree."

Casey could not help laughing at this, but he
made no objection, and I will not deny that at the
moment I would have been quite willing to have
remained with Joe. I had volunteered, however,
to carry a carbine for Casey to use, so I was
bound to accompany him, and was very proud at
being for the first time trusted with arms.

By this time the men had been gone five or ten

minutes, and it was thought that they must have nearly completed the circuit, when suddenly a hound barked hoarsely, and then there was a frightened, inarticulate voice heard, which gradually gathered itself into a negro woman's shriek, coming from between the negro quarters and the house.

"O Marsa Jay, Marsa Jay," it cried, "the Yankees is yere! the Yankees is yere!" and there was a noise of frantic running toward the house. Evidently one of the women slaves in the quarters who was faithful to the interests of the big house had discovered the danger and betrayed us.

"Forward, boys, double quick," cried Casey, leading the way. "Skirmishers close in straight on the house!" and I could hear the order repeated by other officers along the line.

Dark forms became dimly visible amid the standing cotton plants, all pushing their way in the direction of the big house. Meanwhile, we of the reserve were running more directly by the path. The house remained dark, but as we drew near there were bangings of door and voices calling within, and before we had covered more than half the interval angry little spurts of fire began to dart from the closed windows. Two big dogs came bounding down the path toward Casey, who shot one of them with his revolver, while one of the blue jackets spitted the other cleverly upon his sabre bayonet. The barks of defiance changed to howls, and we rushed on.

" Close up to the gallery and fire at the windows ! " was the word, and in another moment a cordon of men was kneeling on the ground, partly concealed from those within by the edge of the low veranda.

The house was a spacious mansion, covering a large area of ground, and the windows, as is the fashion at the South, were all provided with solid wooden shutters. Through these, at a convenient height, augur holes had been bored in view of emergencies, and the lively fire that was kept up at first showed that Hawkson's gang was by no means intimidated by our attack.

The fire of the attacking party was so brisk, however, that it was impossible to remain alive near the window sand the house soon became silent. Word was passed along the line to cease firing, and Casey, prudently taking shelter behind a tree, where I blush to confess I was already in hiding, sung out, " Have you got the back door well guarded, Lawson ? "

" Yes, sir," came from beyond the building.

" Shoot down anybody that attempts to escape."

" Ay, ay, sir."

Just here there was a sharp flash from one of the front windows near at hand, and the bark flew from the tree-trunk close to Casey's head. Half a dozen carbines instantly spoke in reply, and there was a groan and a heavy fall on the floor within the house.

"Hallo, the house," called Casey. "The longer you keep up that kind of thing, the worse it will be for you. I'll give you five minutes to surrender, and then I shall set the house on fire."

Casey rubbed a bunch of matches on the wet sole of his boot, and held the glowing phosphorous against the crystal of his watch, so that he could see the time. All was still within; some of our men took the opportunity to fall back to the shelter of trees near at hand, the better to command the different exits, and the reserve was arranged on both sides of the front steps.

"Four minutes gone," called Casey, and, after a pause that seemed interminable, "Time's up! Are you ready with the fatwood under the house, there?"

"Ay, ay, sir; all ready."

Casey paused, I suppose to give them a moment's grace, but unconditional surrender was a term not included in Jay Hawkson's somewhat limited vocabulary. Without a preliminary sound of warning, the inner bolts shot back, the double doors swung open, and a crowd of dusky figures swarmed out, clearing the veranda at a bound handling their revolvers with deadly facility and dashing away toward the standing timber, each man for himself.

Our blue-jackets and soldiers were prompt enough to respond: the leader of the party, a gigantic fellow with a "live" revolver in each hand, was shot and bayoneted at the same moment as he leaped from the veranda to the ground. Casey, who had sprung forward at the first indication of a rush, had discharged his own revolver as he ran, and the next instant I saw him throw up both hands and reel backward.

Forgetting my own nervousness of a moment before, I jumped to his side, half raising him, so that his head rested on my knee, while the scurrying fight spread itself over the broad lawn and died away with dropping shots in the edge of the timber as the survivors escaped into a tangled undergrowth of palmetto scrub.

Meanwhile, a similar break for liberty had been made from the rear door. Probably there had not been more than fifteen or twenty men in the house altogether, but in the darkness and confusion they looked to be fifty, and, aided by familiarity with the locality, most of them escaped to the woods, leaving one of their number dead on the floor within, another on the lawn, and four wounded in our hands on the ground outside.

Finding that Mr. Casey could not speak, though he was still breathing, and unable in the darkness to locate his wound, I laid him down and shouted for Captain Lawson, who I knew must be within hearing. He came presently, and, sending word to the surgeon, we carried the wounded man into the house, where presently a light was procured and an examination made.

The poor fellow was shot through the head, and was quite unconscious, and, though he breathed for awhile, he could not be resuscitated, and died before we could get him to the boat. The news of this loss quickly spread among the men, and, as it was nearly certain that he had fallen to the pistol of the rebel leader, I thought for a moment that they would break the restraints of discipline and bayonet the wounded man under the surgeon's hands. This big fellow turned out to be Hawkson himself, mortally hurt, but defiant to the last.

We soon found that there were some frightened negresses and three white women in the upper story of the house, and, placing a guard at the foot of the stairs to protect them from possible annoy-ance, we carried their wounded up to them. I shall never forget the ferocity with which those white women regarded us Yankee invaders. Of course it was perfectly natural that they should not be particularly cordial under the circumstances, but such vindictiveness few of us had ever seen on feminine faces before. They asked that Hawkson himself be left to their care, and I really think that if they could have killed him, rather than have him taken away, he would never have left the house alive.

Day was breaking when the last of our men came straggling back in answer to the "recall," and a hasty muster showed seven wounded, two of them quite seriously. Not knowing how soon the enemy might be down upon us in superior force, the boats were brought up to the plantation landing, our dead leader and the wounded carried tenderly aboard, and we started down stream on the first of the ebb.

It had been arranged that the "Otter" should run up the river as soon as there was light enough to clear the bar, and, if possible, capture or destroy the cotton schooners. But we had accomplished our work sooner than was expected, and were on our way down stream before it was broad day. The schooner that lay up stream nearest the scene

of our recent encounter was promptly abandoned
as soon as we were discovered: the guards that
were looked for on board, having no material exis-
tence, and the crews no intention of showing fight.
It was not unlikely that some of her people might
have heard the firing at the plantation as the distance was not too great.   At all events, they made
good time going ashore in a small boat, having first
set the cotton on fire, to prevent its falling into our
hands.

The second cutter, which was ahead, was pretty
close upon their heels, and pulled alongside before
the flames were fairly started.   Scrambling on
board, the men tumbled the blazing bales into the
river.   Fortunately they were lively about it, for a
train had been laid to explode some powder kegs
stowed in the hold.   This disaster was luckily
averted by a Jacky, who saw the loose powder on
deck, and promptly sat down upon it, getting his
skin as well as his trousers scorched by the flash
that came just too late to make mischief.   The
" Otter " thus reckoned another prize to her credit,
in which, however, the " horse marines " were
properly entitled to a share.

When all danger from fire was over, we put a
crew of them on board at their own request, trans-
ferring our killed and wounded to her deck, where

there was more room for their proper bestowal.
The "marines" made sail on her at once, got
under way handsomely, and came bowling down
the river just as the boat flotilla was nearing the
second schooner.

On this craft the work had been more thoroughly
done.   She was burning too fiercely to be approached, so we gave her a wide berth, and she
blew up shortly after we had paused, scattering
a cargo of burning bales over the river, and
presently sinking at her anchorage.   Just below
this we sighted the masts and smokestack of the
"Otter" down toward the bar, and No. 3 schooner
lay still nearer.   No signs of smoke or life were
visible about her, and we could now see that Joe's
description of her deckload of cotton bales had
been correct.

As the "Otter" was coming up the river, and
we could soon join forces with the full crew, it was
decided to let schooner No. 3 severely alone.

"Don't like her looks, nohow, she too still,"
said Joe.   "Look like she play possum."

Accordingly, the boat flotilla sheered off and
went down stream to meet the "Otter."

Not so, however, the temporary captain of
schooner No. 1, whose volunteer crew of soldier-
sailor men was in high spirits at having a sure-

enough sailing craft once more under their feet.   A
young lieutenant of the Eighth Massachusetts was
in command, he having been on two or three voyages
to " the banks " in a Marblehead fisherman.   With
dare-devil recklessness, having a good off-shore
wind on his quarter and all plain sail drawing, he
steered so as to pass within half a cable's length
of the suspicious schooner, going at a great rate.
But for some mysterious reason, or perhaps at
a hint from one of his more experienced crew, his
mind misgave him a bit at the last moment.   He
had the wheel himself, and sharply ordered his
men to take such cover as was afforded by the
cotton bales still remaining on deck.

" Take your rifles with you," he cried, and none
too soon, for the hitherto mythical cotton guard
that we had looked for on the other schooners now
materialized suddenly in the shape of some fifty
gray slouch hats that arose from behind a rampart
of cotton bales placed end to end along the
gunwale of the schooner.   Over these at the same
time were thrust the brown barrels of as many
recently imported English rifles, and a rattling
volley followed the heavy conical bullets, scoring
long white rents across the cotton bales, or striking
with a heavy thud against their perpendicular sides.
Down went the young lieutenant-skipper with a

wound in his thigh, and some of the men who had
not taken warning in time carried away with them
mementos of these deadly Southern riflemen. The
lieutenant was so hard hit that he lost his grip of
the wheel, which went spinning over to port as the
vessel took the bit between her teeth and rounded
to with all her canvas slatting before any one could
jump to take his place.

Fortunately, with a sailor's instinct, the helmsman
had passed to windward of the anchored craft, and,
as the head sails were pretty well sheeted home,
her headway carried her over toward the north
shore of the river, where she took the ground
comfortably, and was evidently berthed there for
the next high tide, unless helped off.

The place where she grounded was a tolerably
long rifle range from the Confederate schooner,
and the crews of the two vessels were very soon
exchanging shots in lively fashion from behind
their respective barricades of cotton bales. Apparently the Confederates had not discovered the
" Otter " coming up when they opened fire on our
prize ; otherwise they might have adopted different
tactics.

The boat flotilla was a half a mile down stream
when all this took place, and the " Otter " a good
mile farther, just making her way into the deep

water of the river inside the bar.   There was a disposition on the part of all hands in the boats to go
back and help defend the prize, but, considering
the situation, there was no need.   Moreover it was
evident that the "horse marines" were able to
defend themselves against any possible boat attack.
So we pulled away as fast as possible to meet the
"Otter," which was feeling her way up the channel.

In ten or fifteen minutes we were alongside, and
in a trice the situation of affairs as between the two
schooners was explained.   This, as may be readily
imagined, had been something of a puzzle to
Captain Ross.   At first he supposed that the
schooner coming down so rapidly under sail was
chasing the boat flotilla, and he was making ready
to fire upon her at long range.   But when the
other schooner opened fire with small arms he saw
that his understanding of the situation was at fault.
All was clear enough now and in three seconds a
big rifled shell went hurtling over the belligerent
schooner and burst in the edge of the woods on
the shore beyond her.

This was accepted as a hint to keep quiet, and
there was a notable falling off in the rapidity of
the rifle practise that had until now been directed
against our prize.   Another shot, better directed,
now that the range had been obtained, struck one

of the cotton bales along the rail, penetrated to its heart before exploding, and filled the air with fluffy white fragments, which flew about the masts and rigging in a cloud, and settled like snow upon the surface of the water.

This settled the question, and we saw that the crew was preparing hastily to abandon the vessel. Why they should do this after so short a defense was a mystery at the time, and it was not until after several hours that it was cleared up. Three big, flat fishing boats had been towing astern, and these were quickly hauled alongside. Into them the gray-clad riflemen tumbled, without standing upon the order of their going, and pulled off for shore with all possible haste. A few rifle shots were sent after them, but to hit a small boat at long range is the rarest luck, and they quickly drew into the mouth of a sheltered creek and disappeared, glad enough, probably, to get away from the well-directed shots that had been howling about their heads.

The "Otter" now ran over as near the prize schooner as she could safely go, and, taking a hawser, succeeded in pulling her off into deep water. Thanks to the efficient protection afforded by the cotton bales, the lieutenant was the only man seriously hurt. He was transferred with the rest of

the wounded to the "Otter," where he could have
better care, and the prize proceeded under sail to
cross the bar and anchor outside awaiting our
arrival and further orders.

This done, we turned our attention to schooner
No. 3, which lay silent and apparently deserted.
Judging from our previous experience with the
others, this vessel also was probably well fitted out
with explosive apparatus and ready to be blown
up. At all events, it would have been the height
of folly to venture aboard of her or even within a
pretty liberal danger line. The "Otter" was
therefore anchored by the stern at a respectful distance, so that she could run for the bar in case of
need without waiting to turn round.

A sharp watch was kept on the schooner, but
no sign of life could be detected, except a large,
brindled, yellow cat, who, after things had quieted
down, made her appearance and walked sedately
all round the rail fore and aft. We had recently
lost our own cat overboard, and in the opinion of
the forecastle such a misfortune is very bad luck.
There was a strong desire on the part of Jacky to
secure this secesh cat as a substitute for our loved
and lost tabby.

"No, boys," Captain Ross said to the deputa-
tion that waited upon him, volunteering to go and

get her; "she isn't worth risking your lives for.
There's something wrong about that schooner.
We will wait awhile, anyhow."

So the forenoon wore away, the tide ebbed,
slackened, turned flood again, and we had to shift
the anchor forward so as to keep headed down
stream.   The wounded were cared for and made
as comfortable as possible, and poor Lieutenant
Casey's body was sewed up in canvas preparatory
to burial at sea as soon as we had made an offing.
This was in accordance with the written request
found among his papers, which bore date of the
day before, and, after giving certain directions
concerning his effects, concluded with these words,
which I copied out for the captain and privately
for my own log book at the same time : —

"Bury me at sea, if anything happens to me
to-night; I don't think I could rest easy in Carolina soil, sacred though it is said to be."

His wishes were respected, for, in fact, we went
to sea that same afternoon, and all hands were
mustered on deck to attend the solemn burial service just before the sun went down.   The customary three volleys were fired as the heavily
shotted canvas plunged overboard, and that was
the last of the most popular officer on the ship.

Soldiers and sailors are very much alike at such

times; they will do anything for a comrade or a shipmate while he is alive, but when he is gone, and the last words have been said, and the last volleys fired, it is to a quick and merry tune that they march back to quarters if on shore, and they are very apt to make extra efforts to pass a jolly evening if they are at sea. Casey was a gallant and able young officer, and the idea that such a life as his had been snuffed out by the hand of a desperado like Hawkson was hard for most of us to endure — especially hard when we knew that our own surgeon was doing all that lay in his power to save this same desperado's life.

But this is a digression. I must return to schooner No. 3, which I left with a big yellow cat standing her watch on deck in dignified solitude. Now, I do not in the least expect anybody to believe what I am going to relate, but I will leave it to any of the "Otter's" crew to expose me if I deviate in the slightest degree from the literal truth.

Nearly the whole of our watch on deck was intently interested in pussy's operations on board the schooner. About the middle of the afternoon she was sitting on the rail basking in the sun, blinking her big yellow eyes as could be seen through a glass, and returning the combined gaze of our crew with interest. A landsman can hardly understand the superstitious awe with which a company of sailor men will become interested in such a seemingly insignificant incident as this. But a great many of the men were really upset by it. They could not bear to go below while pussy was in sight. If they tried to do something that took them away from the post of observation they would come nervously back from time to time to steal a look across the water at their fetish.

It was near the full of the tide when some one cried out, " Look, there's something to pay over there." Pussy had suddenly arched her back and increased the size of her tail to enormous proportions. While we looked she emitted a long-drawn wail, such as a cat only executes when in great agony of mind. Then she fled forward like a yellow streak; leaping over cotton bales and other obstacles, she flashed out on the bowsprit, over the furled headsails, and when she reached the jibboom shot out into the air with another blood-curdling screech, and described a long curve down to the water, beneath which she disappeared. Every sailor man in sight winced at the spectacle, and stood ready to jump overboard and go to the rescue if an opportunity occurred.

" Go and pick her up, if you like," said the

officer of the deck, "but keep well clear of the schooner," and never was one of the "Otter's" boats more quickly manned and away than was the third cutter on this occasion.

Cats hate the water, as everybody knows, and they will not take to it except under great stress of fear or necessity, but they are not bad swimmers when driven to extremity. Pussy had probably recognized through that mystical sense that is known to science as "telepathy" the fact that we were friendly to her on board the "Otter"; at all events, she was making the best time that she could to meet the cutter that was going to meet her, when, without the slightest warning, schooner No. 3 burst asunder amidships, her spars shooting aloft, and her deckload of cotton bales turning somersaults in the air in every direction.

The cutter was pretty well within the danger limit, and the "Otter" herself not far beyond it, but, luckily, no harm was done by the falling fragments, and when the hurly-burly was over, and the great cloud of white smoke was rolling off to seaward before the wind, the cutter took to its oars, and quickly discovered puss seated on a floating bale, very wet and bedraggled, but doing her best to get herself dry and presentable, and ready to start her purring apparatus the instant she found

herself in friendly arms and being rubbed dry
with half the red bandanas in the cutter's crew.

Schooner No. 3, then, was not the comparatively
innocent blockade runner that we had supposed
her to be; but was in reality a powder-boat just
over from Bermuda, and consigned, no doubt, to the
ordnance department of the Southern Confederacy.
We could readily understand now why it was that
her crew had deserted her with such unanimous
alacrity as soon as our shells began to burst on
board. How the explosion was timed we never
found out, but undoubtedly a slow match had been
set intended to burn several hours, and perhaps
some kind of a trap was set besides to hasten
matters in case the vessel was boarded, and thus
prove fatal to a goodly number of the Yankee invaders.

Into the question of pussy's discovery of the
approaching explosion I shall not enter, but will
leave that for those who study into the mysteries
of beasts and birds. As nothing remained to
detain us in the Santee, we got our anchor an hour
after the explosion, and, having performed the last
rites at sea for Lieutenant Casey, went back to our
old anchorage in Georgetown Bay, first putting a
regular crew on board the prize and starting her off
to Boston for adjudication.

One more incident about pussy, who was by common consent named " Santee " as soon as she came aboard.   After she had been well dried by the galley fire, she made an exhaustive inspection of the spar deck from stem to stern, anxiously watched the while by every Jacky who had been at sea long enough to know how much depended upon her conduct.   We had gotten underway by this time and, after making the circuit of the deck, everybody standing respectfully aside so that her meditations should not be disturbed, Santee erected her tail to its full height, walked purring to the man at the wheel, and rubbed herself affectionately against his legs.

Could she possibly have chosen any more dignified or comprehensive way of showing her approval of the ship and its company ?   She could not possibly attempt to rub herself against the legs of some two hundred men ; therefore she selected the one whom her experience as a sea-going cat told her was the most important person on board. Jacky was nearly beside himself with delight, and predicted all sorts of good luck for the " Otter."

Santee did not find her way below decks until after dark, and then, by some mysterious instinct, went almost directly to the sick bay where Hawkson lay dying from his several wounds.   The surgeon's steward on duty outside the open door was awakened from a doze by hearing a terrified yell from his patient, and sprang up to find Santee at the foot of the bunk, her eyes flaming and every individual hair erect. Hawkson had shrunk together, drawing himself up at the head of the bunk with a supreme effort of strength, his eyes dilating with horror, and terror expressed by every lineament of his countenance.

" Take it away, take it away," he cried; " it's that same infernal cat."

The steward seized Santee and put her on deck, but when he returned to his post the slave-driver had passed to his last account. We sent his body ashore at Pilot Town, and buried it decently near the old negro whom he had so cruelly hanged only a few days before. If it was disinterred and given a military funeral after our departure it was none of our concern. We had treated him with more consideration than he deserved, for he had repeatedly violated all laws of civilized warfare.

CHAPTER XIII.

" COME ABOARD, SIR ! "

AN uneventful period of longshore duty followed the Santee expedition, interrupted
about the middle of October, when the supply
steamer brought us with our infrequent mail an
order to join the blockading squadron off Charleston.

On arriving there, we learned that the secret
agents of the government had reported two English
steamers with full cargoes of cotton at the wharves
ready for sea, and intending to make the attempt
to run out together, if possible, on the same night,
so as to confuse the blockading squadron and thus
to favor each other's chances for escape.

Blockade running by steam, and its natural pre-
ventive blockading by steam, were unknown quan-
tities in 1861. Both sides had to learn how.
When Federal gunboats were few in number it
was easy to evade them. But even afterwards,
when a double cordon of gunboats surrounded the
entrances to the principal Confederate ports, block-

ade runners managed to slip through on dark
nights, and would doubtless have continued to do
so, no matter how much the fleet might have been
increased.

There were only three vessels off Charleston at
this time, the "Otter" making the fourth, and,
while we could easily close the direct approaches
during the hours of daylight, dark nights afforded
abundant opportunity for entrance or escape.
Especially was this the case in winter, when
easterly storms made it necessary for the squadron to seek an offing for safety, and here was the
blockade runner's opportunity. If he could once
get outside of the harbor after the sea had mod-
erated, and before the blockading vessels had returned to their stations, he could probably show
his heels to anything that he was likely to meet.

By daylight, even, it was not impossible for
blockade runners of moderate draught to make
their escape, for, besides the regular ship channels
affording direct entrance to Charleston Harbor,
there are numerous creeks and passages among
the marshy islands to the north and south, through
which small vessels can easily work their way at
high tide. The typical blockade runner was not
constructed with a view to any extraordinary degree of sea-worthiness; if she could be made fast

enough to run away from the average gunboat
with a load of cotton, she would pay for herself
several times over on one trip.

There is no complete record of all the successful trips made by blockade runners, but between
the outbreak of hostilities and November, 1865,
nearly one thousand vessels of all kinds, large and
small, were captured by the navy, and of these
something like seventy were steamers, mostly with
valuable cargoes, either of war material, if inward
bound, or of cotton, if outward bound. On one
side the possibility of enormous commercial profits
prompted to daring enterprise, and on the other,
the prospect of liberal prize money was a powerful
incentive to vigilance and effort.

With only four vessels to guard such a harbor
as Charleston, the chances were largely in favor
of the blockade runners, but we did the best we
could with the means at our disposal. , When the
weather promised to be moderate the custom was
for each vessel to lie off the entrance of one of the
channels and send a boat to patrol in the narrower
waters inside the bar, showing a signal in case a
blockader was discovered making her way out.

According to my plan of trying to see all sorts
of service afloat, I succeeded, after several rebuffs,
in getting permission to go on one of these patrol

boats, where boys were not generally wanted. But
by promising to make myself useful I got permission to go at last.

It was a very dark night, with a light breeze
blowing in from sea, so that noises were carried inland rather than seaward. It was, indeed, an almost
ideal night for blockade runners to try their chances
at slipping out. Four ships' boats do not make
much of a show on a dark night in the wide harbor
mouth, so we did not attempt to keep up regular
communication, but there was a general understanding that each boat should watch its own
channel, and let the others take care of themselves.
Now, there are, or were then, four channel entrances
to the harbor practicable for blockade runners;
two of these,— the North Channel and the Swash,
— were practically one, being separated merely by
small, island-like shoals.

At this double channel we were stationed, in
company with a boat from one of our consorts.
The night wore silently on, the men now and then
pulling a few strokes to keep the boat from drifting
into the breakers, but for the most part resting on
their oars and keeping absolute silence.

The regulation lights of the coast had long since
been extinguished, but the Confederates kept certain range lights burning for the benefit of chance

visitors, it being well understood among them what the bearings were so that a pilot familiar with the coast could find his way in on the darkest night.

These were the only signs of life to be seen, for on the blockading squadron outside none of the usual lights were shown, and all those that were absolutely necessary below decks were carefully screened.

It was pretty well past midnight when I awoke from a chilly doze into which I had dropped in my place next to the bow oar. Everybody was on the alert, the men grasping their oars and ready for instant action.

"What's up?" I whispered to the man next me.

"Listen," was his only reply.

Certainly something was astir somewhere up the harbor, and, listening intently, I presently recognized it as the beat of slowly revolving paddle wheels. Nearly all the blockade runners were side wheelers; the screw propeller had not then come into such universal use as at present. It was the policy of out-going steamers in still weather to run slowly, so as to make as little noise as possible until they were actually discovered; then they would go ahead full speed and trust to luck and skill to make good their escape. These paddles that we heard could not be very far distant, for the wind was against our hearing anything from that direction; therefore every eye was strained to discover the first signs of the approaching vessel.

Orders in regard to boat's signals varied from time to time as experience suggested change, but on this occasion we were provided with the ordinary blue lights used in sea service, which were to be displayed as soon as it was certain that a steamer was coming out. It would not do to show the light too soon, for the approaching vessel might be an armed steam patrol boat of the enemy, too strong for us to fight and too fleet for us to escape, so there was nothing for it but to keep still and await developments.

Some one like Pilot Joe would have been very welcome to our boat just at this time; he could probably have seen what was coming, but, strain our eyes as we would, nothing could as yet be discovered; and still the steady beat of paddles became more and more distinct, till with the intensity of listening the senses became confused and one could not be at all sure from which direction the sound came.

But we had not long to wait, for presently there was a flash of light from the other side of the channel, where our companion boat was supposed to be stationed. She had evidently discovered a

blockade runner, and let off her signal.   Our own
coxswain was in the act of following suit, without
waiting for further evidence, when one of the
waist oarsmen sung out, " Give way all, quick !
Here she is right on top of us."

At the same instant we heard a jingle of bells
rung somewhere in the darkness, and an instantane-
ous churning of paddle wheels beating the water
furiously showed that the signal had been given
to go ahead at full speed.   Another moment, and
from my place forward I saw the lift of a black
bow almost over my head, and then, before a
stroke could be pulled, there came a mighty crash,
as a sharp cutwater struck us amidships, cutting
the boat clean in two, and tossing the crew off,
part to one side and part to the other.   The fragments of the boat, borne down by the rushing mass
of the big ship went under, and every man with
them.   Whether any of them escaped or not,
beside myself, I knew not for a long time.

I was a good swimmer and thoroughly at home
in the water, and the first instinctive thought that
flashed through my brain was, " I must dodge the
paddle wheel ! " and, turning head downward, I
swam toward the bottom for all I was worth.   A
chance kick against the ship's side as she swept by
helped me a little, and I was presently aware of a

seething and roaring in my ears that led me to think the danger was past. At all events, my supply of breath was nearly gone, and I rose to the surface, half strangled, throwing out my arms wildly, probably with the insane instinct of a drowning man to catch at a straw.

I saw nothing, knew nothing, until I found myself hanging on grimly by a rope that had fallen within reach, and upon which my grasp had desperately tightened. With the instinct of a sailor, I had climbed a little way till nearly clear of the water, which was rushing past at great rate just below me and swashing against my legs occasionally as the ship rolled.

This was the first thing that I noticed as my senses gathered themselves together after a few seconds of confusion under water. The rope hung slack, being, in fact, one of the lighter mooring lines that had not yet been hauled inboard, and by taking a turn around it with my leg, and another with one of my arms, I was enabled to hang suspended without making much effort, while I caught my breath and blew the salt water out of my nose and mouth. In a few seconds life and consciousness began to assert themselves, and I knew that I must make a mighty effort to climb on deck before my strength left me altogether.

Blockade runners had very little free-board, as a rule, and this one was no exception; that is to say, it was only a few feet from the water line to the deck, and by summoning all my strength and resolution I went up hand over fist with the assistance of my feet against the ship's side. This is a very easy thing for a sailor to do when he is in his right mind and with dry clothing, but it is by no means so easy when one has just escaped death by drowning and is wet and exhausted.

I finally reached the rail and tumbled over, not caring where I fell, so long as it was not overboard.

By good luck I came down on a cotton bale, for she carried a deckload, and lay still, panting and nearly in a swoon.

But during these few terrible moments the " Palma "— for that was her name — had been speeding seaward, and was now in the swing of the breakers on the bar. I took no heed of my surroundings, and may have been actually unconscious for a little, but it could not have been long, for I was brought to myself by the stunning report of a heavy gun close at hand and the whoop of a shell that seemed to pass close overhead. This reacted upon me like an electric shock; my heart began to beat, the blood started through my veins

again, and I felt the warmth of returning life ting-
ling in my limbs.

Bang! Whizz! Another shell! And this brought
me up. By kneeling on my cotton bale I could
look over the rail and partly see what was going
on; judging from the flash of the guns, I knew
that all four of the blockading squadron were in
it; but evidently there were two points of attack,
—that is to say, two escaping steamers.

Two of the gunboats, which I judged to be the
"Otter" and the "Monticello," were firing at us,
serving their pivot rifles with great rapidity and, it
seemed to me, with a most uncomfortable accuracy
of practise.

It makes a wonderful difference whether one is
behind a gun or in front of it, in estimating the
skill of the gunner. Hitherto, in my limited experience of naval actions, I had been safe behind
the breach of the best guns. Now the case was
different. I was on an unarmed blockade runner,
fleeing for her life, as it were, out into the blackness of the open sea, and my old shipmates were
pounding away at me with six-inch projectiles, as
though my life was not of the slightest consequence.

Now and then a shell would crash through the
woodwork somewhere, but the solid mass of cotton

that well-nigh filled the entire ship protected its vul-
nerable points, and the machinery was uninjured.
It was very soon evident that we were distancing
our pursuers, and from the manner in which the
other gunboats were firing I judged that our sister
fugitive was likewise making good her escape.

I had tumbled on board at a point pretty well aft,
and at a time when the eyes of all on deck were
naturally directed forward toward the blockading
fleet. All was dark except the binnacle light, and
that was carefully screened. No one had seen
me. But now, as we came abreast of the fleet,
men came tramping aft, and I thought it best to
lay low.

Knowing from experience that I should be
pretty sure to find a warm place near the machinery, I jumped down from my cotton bale,
without any attempt at concealment, and walked
forward to where I could see the black column of
smoke made partially visible by an intermingled
cloud of escaping sparks as it poured out from the
big smoke-stack. One figure was not to be dis-
tinguished from another in the darkness, and,
though I brushed against some of my new shipmates in passing, I was not molested, and soon
reached the clear space about the engines amid-
ship.

Feeling about in the darkness, I presently discovered a sheltered nook behind a boxlike chest, and in the lee of some sort of a steam box that afforded a comfortable degree of heat, where I should be in no danger of discovery before daylight, except by accident. The temperature was a good deal like that of a Turkish bath, but I knew it was best for me to get dry and keep warm during the process, so I disposed myself as comfortably as I could, and listened to the shots and to the exploding shells as they grew fainter and fainter in the distance, till at last they ceased altogether, and at about the same time, I suppose, I dropped off into an exceedingly sound sleep.

It was broad daylight when I awoke; the sun was streaming across the deck, with its rows of cotton bales, and the dark shadows of spars and rigging were swaying to and fro on the deck as the ship rolled in the trough of the sea. I could tell from the motion that we were going at a high rate of speed; the engines were throbbing away as hard as ever.

For awhile I could not remember what had happened, but when I put up my hand to feel for my blue cloth sailor cap the whole thing suddenly came back, and I remembered that my cap must have gone when I was under water, and here I

was on a swift blockade runner, headed, no doubt,
either for Bermuda or Nassau. Was I a deserter,
or a prisoner of war, or what? My knowledge of
maritime law was too limited to enable me to decide
the question offhand.

The night before I had been too much shaken to
give any thought to the situation, but now I was
dry and warm, and I should presently be hungry,
and, although not yet discovered, it was necessary
to decide at once upon some course of action. So,
sitting up in the little cubby-hole, I made shift to
wash my hands and face, wetting the corner of
my bandanna handkerchief in some hot water that
dripped from a steam joint near by. Then I
brushed the white salt from my dark blue jacket
and trousers, adjusted my knife-lanyard as well as I
could, crawled out of my hiding-place, and stood up.

Not a soul was in sight, but the sun was warm,
and I caught a glimpse of blue white-crested waves
over the rail as the vessel rolled. I stamped and
kicked the cramps out of my legs, still remaining
by the smoke-stack, for I cared not in the least
now how soon I was discovered. Two men came
along presently on their way aft and stared rather
sharply as they went by, but they said nothing. I
suppose they were stokers or deck-hands and took
me, perhaps, for one of the passengers whom they

had not seen before. Blockade runners often carried passengers back and forth between ports, so that my presence on board was easily to be explained on this supposition.

On completing my toilet to reasonable satisfaction, I sauntered forward, bareheaded, with my hands in the pockets of my reefer, to the forward windlass, where the officer on the bridge could see me, and I him. Facing about, I looked up, but he was gazing intently through his marine glass at something on the horizon. I did not know at the time, but found out afterward, that he was the captain, and an officer in the British navy, who had been granted leave of absence to pursue temporarily the lucrative profession of blockade running. Presently he laid the glass down in its canvas pocket and turned in my direction. As soon as I caught his eye I saluted, navy fashion, and reported, "Come aboard, sir."

He was a stout, florid Englishman, wearing a navy tunic with gold lace on the sleeves, very likely one of his old service uniforms. He looked hard at me, rubbed his eyes, looked again, and leaned his elbows on the bridge rail for a still better look.

"Yes, I see you have," he said at length; "but who are you?"

"If you please, sir, may I come up on the

"COME ABOARD, SI"

bridge? I'd like to speak to you in private." For
by this time several of the forecastle hands were
standing around.

"No, I'll come down to you. Mr. Sawyer, it's
your watch, I believe; you may take charge."

"Now, then, youngster, what is it?" he said,
when we had reached a place out of earshot from
the others.

"My name is John Benson, sir," I said. "I am
a naval apprentice of the United States gunboat
'Otter,' and I wish to surrender as a prisoner of
war."

I knew very well that there were no naval
apprentices in the service at that time, but it
sounded better than "first-class boy."

"Bless my soul! How did you get aboard?"

I told him briefly of the disaster to the patrol boat
on the preceding night and of my miraculous
escape. He looked utterly incredulous.

"Show me that line," he said, after reflecting a
moment. So I led him aft to the rail where I had
climbed over, and there, sure enough, was the rope
that had saved me.

"Well, me lad," the captain said, the incredulous expression passing off from his good-natured
countenance, "do you know I begin to believe
you're not lying?"

"Indeed, I'm not, sir," I replied, flushing a little, I suppose; "I don't know what other proof I can offer you. Oh, yes," I said, a sudden thought striking me. "We got a mail from the North only a few days ago, and I believe I have some letters in my pocket."

So I fished them out. They were all soaked with salt water, the stamps gone, and the ink blurred, but they satisfied the captain's doubt, and he turned me over to a steward with orders to make me comfortable in the second cabin. This I found to mean that I was to mess with the petty officers of the ship, which was all that could be reasonably expected.

The tale of my arrival on board soon spread in various forms of exaggeration, and when the call came for breakfast I found myself the butt of plenty of good-natured and some ill-natured chaff. There were a few Southerners and secessionists aboard, who, after the manner of their kind, were incapable of the courtesies of civilized warfare, and these, taking advantage of my lonely and unprotected condition, to say nothing of my comparatively small size and few years, did not hesitate to say all the ugly things they could about the Federal Government. I hit back to some extent, but upon the whole they were too many for me, so eventually it was the best policy to hold my peace.

Most of my fellow voyagers, however, were Englishmen, who cared very little about our national quarrel so long as it afforded them the high pay and good fare current on blockade runners. The captain sent for me toward evening, after he had his nap and recovered from his exciting, all-night vigil, and cross-examined me about my adventure, — how the patrol boats had been disposed in the channel, how far outside the gunboats were, and so on, gradually approaching the subject of the general disposition of the blockading squadron. Boylike, I did not immediately understand what he was driving at, but it occurred to me before he got very far, and I could not help laughing a little when his purpose became evident.

"Beg pardon, sir," I said; "I've been telling you the truth so far; but if you follow up that line of questions I shall have to begin to lie more or less."

The captain looked rather taken aback at this, and flushed up to the roots of his sandy hair; but, after clearing his throat once or twice, and hesitating a little, he blurted out with, "Quite right, too, me lad, quite right; but think it over a bit, and perhaps this will decide you to help me out."

He took a gold sovereign from his vest pocket and laid it on the table. I had never seen one before, and, my curiosity being aroused, naturally asked what it was and how much it was worth. Overcoming the natural astonishment of a British subject at the idea that any living being can be ignorant of the value of one of Her Majesty's coins, he condescendingly told me that it was worth about five dollars in American money. Then it dawned upon me what he was giving me the money for.

"Captain," said I, "I've a good notion to put this into my pocket, and then lie to you about the fleet all the same. I could do it easy enough. Oh, yes, I could give you a beautiful plan of my own for managing the blockading squadron, but it wouldn't be at all like the one that the officer in command off Charleston is at present carrying out. They say that all is fair in war, but I expect to be an officer in the navy some day, and we don't do that kind of thing in our service."

I laid the coin down, and he put it in his pocket, his face once more growing very red as he said : —

"I ask your pardon, me lad; indeed, I do. You see I've been associating with these secesh fellows so much lately that I've got to think no

Yankee has so much as a streak of honesty in him. But I honor you for it, me lad; I do, indeed. And let me ask you, have you thought what you will do after we get to Bermuda? We shall be there inside of a day and a half, I hope. Have you thought what you will do?"

"Well, sir, I'd like to ask your advice about that. I suppose that if there is a Yankee gunboat in port I might report on board. But if not, I should think the American consul might take charge of me."

"I'd be glad to take you back with me," he said, "but there might be a little awkwardness. I'm afraid they would hang you for a spy if they caught you in Charleston."

"That would be unpleasant, certainly."

"Well, there's no special hurry; we'll see how the land lays after we get to Bermuda."

All the way across the Gulf Stream we had fine, sunshiny weather, with an ugly lop of a sea, to be sure, the discomfort of which was somewhat increased by the high rate of speed at which we ran. Our course was somewhat crooked, too, for every vessel that we saw was a possible Yankee gunboat and had to be given a wide berth.

As we sighted the hilltops of the little tropical island on the morning of the third day and began to draw in toward the land, we made out a steamer to the northward, hull down beyond the horizon, but burning soft coal and steering a nearly parallel course. On inspection she proved to be our sister fugitive of Charleston bar, and we steamed into the lovely land-locked harbor almost side by side.

There was a great commotion in the sleepy little seaport that was just awakening from its century of lethargy to a short era of unwonted prosperity. The dazzlingly white houses sat among their orange trees on the sloping hillsides and made a wonderfully beautiful setting for the sparkling waters of the harbor. The whole population, apparently, turned out upon the unprecedented occasion of seeing two cotton-laden steamers come into port. Every one who could beg, borrow, or steal a boat got into it, and a great fleet of miscellaneous craft surrounded us as we let go our anchors. Not a few negroes even swam out to us from the shore, and all of them were yelling and in a high state of excitement.

After the necessary official preliminaries, great gangs of negroes were put to work breaking out the cargo and, as soon as there was any room, reloading the empty space with all kinds of arms and munitions of war. All was confusion and hurry, half-naked negroes tumbling over one another and over

cotton bales in their haste to earn the high wages
that they were enabled to ask.

The poor, lonely little Yankee sailor boy was
for the time forgotten. Along toward evening,
however, he began to think it was high time for
such an important character as a prisoner of war to
be remembered. So he stood around in the neighborhood of the captain till he caught his eye, and
asked permission to go ashore and see the consul.

" Why, bless me soul," cried the captain
heartily; " I had forgotten all about the boy.
Yes, to be sure. And I'll go with you. I suppose
the consul will take me word as a gentleman,
even if I *am* a blockade runner."

We were set ashore in a boat, and a short walk
took us to the consulate, where my heart gave a
foolish little jump when I saw the stars and stripes
floating over the door. The consul listened to my
story and the captain's confirmation thereof, and
was kind enough to say that I came fairly within
his jurisdiction. He agreed, moreover, to provide
me with board and lodging and send me home by
the next opportunity, for such is the duty of United
States consuls toward seamen in distress all over
the world.

So I took leave of my friend, the English
captain, thanking him for his kindness. Some-

what to my astonishment, he offered his hand
at parting, and said, after a moment's hesitation : —

"Here, me lad, take this as a loan if you like ; I
know you must be a bit short of pocket money,"
and he dropped a sovereign into the pocket of my
reefer, turned on his heel, and strode abruptly
away, leaving me, as you may well think, somewhat taken aback at this act of generosity.

An examination of the shipping list showed
that there was nothing bound for a Northern
port for nearly three weeks, so I made the best of
it, and, after loafing about and seeing the town
and its surroundings until I was tired, told the
consul that I should die of idleness if he could not
give me something to do. He laughingly said
that I had better learn to be a gentleman of leisure
while I had the opportunity, but made no objection,
so I, with my British gold, bought a hickory
shirt and a pair of overalls, found a job as a
stevedore, and put by quite a snug little sum
before the bark on which my passage was engaged
was ready to sail for New York.

On reaching port, I hurried to a telegraph
office — they were not so plenty in those days
as they are now — and wired Uncle Abner as fol-
lows : —

*Picked up by blockade runner that ran us down.
Bermuda. Rejoin " Otter " at once. Have
written.   Jack.*

Then I posted the letter already written, for I
knew that I must have been mourned as lost by
my friends at Rockledge.

Reporting at the Brooklyn Navy Yard, I presented my certificate from the United States consul at Bermuda, and told my story to an official at
the commandant's office, who evidently thought
that both I and the consul were endeavoring to
impose upon him. However, he allowed himself
to be convinced at last, and gave me transporta-
tion on a supply ship that was on the point of
sailing for Hampton Roads, where, after waiting a
few days, I was forwarded to the " Otter," still
on blockading duty off Charleston.

Of course, I had been given up for lost, with
more than half the crew of the patrol boat. Four
of my boat-mates, as I now learned, had been
picked up by the other patrol, who had heard their
cries for help after the blockade runners had passed
out to sea.

It was after dark when I was run alongside the
" Otter " in a ship's boat, and one of my old mess-
mates was holding the lantern at the port gangway

as I climbed the ladder. When I addressed him by name, and he saw me emerging from the darkness, he staggered backward in sheer terror, thinking a ghost was come aboard, and nearly knocked over the officer on watch, who stood a little behind him. It was some minutes before I could convince anybody that I was myself, and then nothing would do but I must be taken straight to the captain.

It will be remembered, perhaps, that I had done some clerk's work for Captain Ross. Indeed, he had treated me as kindly as a commanding officer can properly treat a ship's boy in the navy. At any rate, the watch officer walked me aft and into the captain's quarters with as little ceremony as possible. Collaring me as we entered, he pushed me forward with : —

"Beg pardon, captain. Here's a deserter just come aboard. Thought you might like to order him shot at once."

The captain looked up from the book that he was reading, and did not recognize me at first, but, as I came forward toward the light, and he saw who it was, he threw down his book and jumped up.

"What, Benson?" he cried. "Why, you young rascal, where have you been? You're drowned according to the articles of war. I made out your final statement myself and sent your traps home. The boy's an impostor; take him for'ard, Trevor!" —this to the watch officer. "What do you mean by bringing him here?"

All this was delivered with an air of severity that actually frightened me, and I was for retreating as speedily as possible, but Trevor, who knew his commander's ways better than I did, replied:—

"Very good, sir. I thought you might want to put him in irons, sir. Come along, Benson."

I heard Captain Ross blowing his nose violently as we turned, and just as we reached the door he called out, "Here, confound it all, where are you going? Come back; I want to talk to you."

So back I went, and when Trevor had closed the door behind him Captain Ross shook hands with me in a way that I am sure was quite contrary to good order and naval discipline, and made me recount my adventures from beginning to end.

"And you didn't take time to run up to Stony-haven?" he asked when I had finished.

"No, sir, but I telegraphed, and reported back as soon as I could."

"That was right; but, really, you deserve a few days' leave, and I will see that you get it."

"Thank you, sir! You're very good, but if

you don't mind I'd like to stay by the ships. I hear there is an expedition fitting out."

" And you think your luck will stand by, do you? Well, we'll see about that. Anyhow, I shall detail you for special service again."

After I was dismissed, another and more boisterous welcome awaited me for'ard of the main-mast, and at last I was glad enough to turn in and make believe go to sleep in my old hammock.

During my absence a great naval victory had been won at Port Royal (Nov. 7, 1861), in which nearly the whole fleet had taken part, the heavier armed vessels steaming past the forts again and again, and reducing them to silence after a bombardment of a few hours. This victory secured what was, in fact, the object of the expedition,— a harbor available as a naval rendezvous south of Cape Hatteras. A strong armed garrison was immediately placed in the captured forts, and the position proved to be of the greatest value in maintaining the efficiency of the blockade. The headquarters of the South Atlantic Squadron was soon afterward removed from Hampton Roads to this place.

I could not but regret having missed the imposing spectacle of this action, especially as the

"Otter" had borne an honorable, if not particularly prominent part in the engagement.

But I was destined to still another disappointment, for the "Otter" had seen so much hard service that an overhauling was deemed absolutely necessary, so just before the Roanoke expedition in February, 1862, we were ordered to Brooklyn to go into dry dock, and, although a considerable number of our officers and men were transferred to other vessels, I found Captain Ross inexorable, so made the best of it, took my promised leave of absence, and passed a luxurious fortnight at Rockledge.

Returning to Brooklyn on the expiration of my leave, I found that the "Otter" had been ordered out of commission, and was undergoing a thorough overhauling, her crew being dispersed to the four corners of the earth, or, at least, of the navy. I tried to find Captain Ross, but he had applied for a new command, so I had to sling my hammock in the receiving ship and await orders, which presently came, assigning me to a draft for the "Minnesota," still lying in Hampton Roads, waiting for the appearance of her twin sister, the "Merrimac," disguised as an ironclad.

CHAPTER XIV.

IRON AGAINST WOOD.

IT was with a sinking of the heart which I would not have admitted on any account that I found myself, after a short voyage from New York, once more nearing the same "Minnesota" at which I had gazed with such feelings of awe a few months before. In a way, it would be a fine thing to be counted as one of the crew of the big warship, but, on the other hand, I should have to take my chances in new surroundings, in a crowd probably of very rough boys and rougher men, and fight my battles all over again. However, I put on as bold a face as I could, shouldered my dunnage, climbed the gangway, and stood with my shipmates, ranged along in the waist by the mainmast, while we were assigned our mess numbers and turned over to our respective division officers.

On one point, at least, I could congratulate myself. I should become familiar with all the forms of naval routine on a large scale. The "Minnesota" carried a crew of about seven hundred men,

all told, with a full marine guard, a fine band of
music, and all the pomp and circumstance of a
flag officer's official residence. On the little
" Otter," while perfect discipline and punctilious
naval etiquette were maintained, there was always
a feeling that she was merely a makeshift man-of-
war, well enough in her own way, but not the real
thing, after all. But here on the " Minnesota,"
with her wide, white decks, her high bulwarks,
lofty spars, and tremendous battery of heavy guns,
there was a general air of solidity that gave one
the satisfaction of knowing that she, indeed, was
the finest ship of her class afloat.

This was all very fine, but there were rumors
abroad among the blue-jackets between decks, as
well as among the wardroom officers and in the
flag officer's cabin, to the effect that just beyond
the low point that we could see so plainly from our
topgallant forecastle, a strange craft was fitting out
that would, before long, make her appearance and
try conclusions with the fleet.

This vessel has already been referred to,— the
" Merrimac,"— a sister ship to the " Minnesota,"
which had been sunk and partly destroyed in April
(1861), by order of Commodore Macauley, when
the Norfolk Navy Yard was abandoned. It was
known early in the summer that she had been raised

and floated into the dry dock in a comparatively uninjured condition as to her machinery and lower hull; that she had been rechristened "The Virginia," and that an accomplished officer of the old navy, Lieutenant John M. Brooke, was superintending the work of converting her into the most formidable ironclad afloat.

"Contrabands" now and then strayed into the lines, and were interviewed by "Jackies" when on shore leave, who had seen this monster and described her with all the exuberance of the African imagination, aided and abetted by a sublime disregard of fact. Naturally, being on the spot, we heard more about this unknown foe than we did about a certain little craft that was being hastily knocked together at the North.

The Confederates deserve all the credit of having led off in the matter of ironclads. No sooner were they satisfied of their naval inferiority in quantity than they went to work making good the deficiency in quality. Hardly had the Norfolk Navy Yard fallen into their hands before they began straining every nerve to produce a single ship that should be able not only to sink the entire Yankee fleet, but could go to sea and lay the great Northern cities under tribute.

Now, in February, it was tolerably certain, from

all information gathered, that she was nearly ready
to come out, and yet so contradictory were the
rumors, so peaceful the broad estuary in which
we lay at anchor in our strength, that we were
half inclined to think that she was altogether a
myth of the imagination. There was plenty of
speculation, however, about the chances, and general sentiment among the blue-jackets was, "Let
her come; we can run her down and send her to
the bottom, even if we can't lick her in a stand-up
fight."

The soft Virginia spring came on apace, and I
had been shaken down into an insignificant niche
as a "first-class boy," a small atom of the great
fighting machine that in those days passed for a
battle ship. Very different she was, of course,
from the steel-clad battle ships of to-day, but highly
efficient, for all that, to meet the conditions for which
she was designed, with her fifty heavy broadside
guns, her hundred-pounder rifles at bow and stern,
and her superb crew of seven hundred men.

To the stern chaser I had been assigned as powder boy at general quarters, and there would be
my station in case of an engagement. I had
become quite attached to the big, polished, brown
creature that could send a pointed iron bolt four or
five miles, and was yet so docile in the hands of

her well-trained crew. My duty for the most part
was to pass cartridges, fill buckets of water, lend a
hand with the gun tackles, and, in short, do anything and everything that my strength was equal
to.

March came in very lamblike, not in the least
resembling the March of a year before on the wild
New England coast, and a week passed by without any farther news of the threatened attack.
The Federal fleet lay as it had lain for months,
with the exception of occasional expeditions for
maneuvering or target practise. It consisted of the
big steam frigates " Minnesota " and " Roanoke,"
sister ships originally to the now transformed " Merrimac." These two lay near Fortress Monroe, and
the old-fashioned sailing frigates, " Congress " and
" Cumberland," were anchored some five miles
above, off the camps at Newport News, where they
could command, or at least threaten, the mouth of
James River with their batteries.

Saturday, the eighth of March, 1862, was a
lovely spring day in Hampton Roads. There had
been lately a severe storm, and our canvas was
shaken out to dry in the warm sunshine, besides
which a goodly part of the week's wash hung on
long lines among the rigging. Most of the boats
were in the water alongside, and the fleet looked as

peaceful as it was possible for warships to look
when practically they are in the presence of the
enemy and are supposed to be ready on the instant
for any emergency.

As with us so with our sister ship, the
"Roanoke," lying further down the Roads, and the
old-fashioned sailing frigate "St. Lawrence," just
in from sea. So, too, with the "Congress" and
"Cumberland," off the mouth of the James, with
Federal shore batteries at Newport News.

In the James River, beyond the reach of our
guns, lay three Confederate gunboats that had come
down on a reconnoitering expedition, but their
presence caused no uneasiness; they often came
down on such expeditions and sometimes indulged
in a little target practise at long range. That they
now made a longer stay than usual near the mouth
of the river did not cause any especial anxiety,
though it might well have suggested the intention
which was presently carried out.

But our Confederate neighbors in the direction
of Norfolk were stirring, too, on this bright spring
morning. A little before noon two more gunboats
made their appearance in Elizabeth River. That
made five in all, and, on our part, the "Zouave," a
small gunboat, was sent off post-haste to investigate. Hardly was she under way when a sixth

and more formidable-looking trail of smoke became
visible above the woods. And the lookout in our
crosstrees presently announced that a large steamer
was coming down.

She moved steadily down stream, attended by the
two smaller steamers, and our little "Zouave"
gunboat pluckily ran up within range and banged
away at her for a few minutes without eliciting any
reply. The big black monster came steadily on,
evidently caring no more for thirty-two-pounder shot
bolts than she did for so many marbles.

The little "Zouave" was not worth wasting
powder upon when larger game was in sight.
Like a little terrier that suddenly discovers that he
has been barking at a sleepy but dangerous mastiff,
the "Zouave" turned and fled back to her consorts.
In justice to her, however, it should be added that
she was recalled by signal from the flagship.

And now the lazy, peaceful-looking Federal
fleet started out of its seeming lethargy in a
twinkling. Down came the long clothes-lines on
deck, and "Jacky's" week's washing was hastily
bundled out of the way and tossed below as the
decks were cleared for action. Top-men lay
aloft to furl the sails, boat-booms were swung in,
and the boats hoisted to their davits or dropped
astern. The magazines were opened, and ammuni-

tion hurried on deck and laid in rows between the guns, ready for instant use.

To a landsman everything seems in hopeless confusion at such a time and every man on the point of tumbling over his mate. But on board a well-ordered ship it is a disciplined and orderly confusion. In a few minutes every man is at his station, quiet reigns fore and aft, and until action begins an order can be heard from one end of the ship to the other.

By the time we were fairly ready the cause of all this commotion became visible from the deck, slowly emerging from behind the wooded lowlands of the Virginia shore, an uncanny shape pushing out into the open waters of the sound. The long-talked-of Merrimac was no longer a myth! Very material, very black and formidable she looked, moving slowly down the Elizabeth Channel. To the naked eye at that distance she was like the roof of a long barn, with its eaves in the water. A nearer view showed rounded, sloping ends in place of gables, and long, low decks just awash with the sea, extending fore and aft beyond the sloping armor plates. A lofty smoke-stack, several port-holes closed with heavy shutters, and some light davits, stays, and the like were alone visible outside of the solid structure.

Slowly she came on down the river channel, and, reaching the deep water of the Roads, turned to the left toward the sailing frigates off Newport News. The " Congress " was nearest to her course, and would apparently be the first to feel the weight of the enemy's metal, but here came in one of the strange incidents of this fight. The commanding officer of the " Virginia " (" Merrimac "), Captain Franklin Buchanan, late of the United States Navy, had a brother who had remained loyal to the Union, and was at this time an officer on board the " Congress." The two brothers may have looked into each other's eyes through marine glasses from the decks of the hostile ships. Certainly each knew that the other was present.

Whether for this or for some other reason, Buchanan merely delivered a broadside in passing, and went on to test his ram on the " Cumberland." His four broadside guns were well aimed and caused destruction on board the " Congress," which, of course, replied with her full battery as long as they could be brought to bear. But her nine-inch solid shot glanced from the iron plates like hailstones from a tin roof, and the " Virginia" passed on, heading straight for the " Cumberland " which lay a few hundred yards beyond.

The old wooden sloop of war began pounding

away with her heavy guns, in anticipation of closer
quarters and in the hope that by a lucky shot her
formidable antagonist might in some way be disabled. But under a full head of steam the
" Virginia " came on, and struck her helpless
victim just by the fore rigging, crashing through
her oaken ribs into her hold, and making a fatal
gash in her side.

But the walls of the gallant old ship nipped
hard, so hard, indeed, that they bit off the
destroyer's nose, and the " Virginia's " iron ram
remained in the opening it had made when she
backed off. It was evident that the " Congress "
could only remain afloat for a short time, but, refus-
ing Buchanan's demand for surrender, Lieutenant
Norris continued to fight his sinking ship, which
soon began to settle by the head.

The lower decks were flooded, gun after gun
had to be abandoned, the wounded were removed
to save them from drowning, and still the fight
went on. Now that their powerful consort was
engaged, the Confederate gunboats came out from
the James River and joined the fight.

More than a hundred of the " Cumberland's "
crew were already killed or wounded, but the men
continued to work their guns till the decks were
awash, and when the word was given, " Every man

for himself," the upper battery was still in action, with the water washing around the wheels of the gun carriages. It was half past three in the afternoon when she gave a lurch to port and went down with her flags all a-flying. More than a third of her crew were killed, or wounded, or drowned in trying to escape to shore.

Seeing that the fate of the "Cumberland" would inevitably be his, Lieutenant Smith, commanding the frigate "Congress," set his head sails, taking advantage of a light breeze, and, aided by the gunboat "Zouave," ran his ship ashore under the guns of the land batteries, where he was at least safe from ramming.

But the "Virginia" was in no especial hurry. She steamed off up the Roads, turned leisurely round, and in half an hour came back to a position where, with the assistance of her consort, she could knock her second victim to pieces at her leisure.

The "Congress" replied with such of her guns as could be brought to bear, but Lieutenant Smith, the commander, was soon killed, and Lieutenant Pendergast, upon whom the command devolved, continued the fight until his ship was on fire in several places and his two principal guns disabled by the enemy's shot. Then he reluctantly hauled down his flag, and the light draft Confederate gunboats came alongside, and began carrying off the crew as prisoners.

The shore batteries, however, did not understand the situation, and firing went on until, in the smoke and confusion, all escaped who were left alive, and the frigate was wrapped in flames from end to end. At about this time Captain Buchanan, of the "Virginia," and one of his officers were wounded by a rifle shot from the shore, and the command fell to Lieutenant Jones.

While this spirited fight was in progress, where was the "Minnesota"? Hard and fast aground, a mile and a half from the scene of action! It has since turned out that her pilot was a traitor and in the pay of the Confederacy,* and that he purposely ran the "Minnesota" aground in compliance with instructions previously received from Richmond.

But the "Virginia" herself was aground more than once during the fight, and the "Roanoke" and "St. Lawrence" had gone ashore, too, on their way to take part in the engagement, so that the blame cannot fairly be laid upon one pair of shoulders.

We of the "Minnesota" saw the "Congress" in flames and the "Cumberland" sunk, and even I, boy as I was, knew that it would be our turn

(* See Maclay's History of the United States Navy, Vol. II., page 295.)

next, if there was daylight enough left for them to
finish us, a task which they seemed quite ready to
undertake.   But on attempting to come to close
quarters they found that the water was so shoal that
it must needs be a duel at long range.

It was a one-sided affair while it lasted, for we
were fixed firmly in the mud, and our enemy could
choose his own position where our most powerful
guns could not be brought to bear upon him.   The
lighter draught gunboats, too, could take position
where they chose in the comparatively shallow
water, and annoy us at their ease.

Captain Van Brunt, who was in command in the
temporary absence of the flag officer, made every
preparation for setting his ship on fire and aban-
doning her rather than surrender, but in the meantime he kept up the fight as well as he could, using
the big pivot rifle forward against the " Virginia,"
while the stern chaser kept the light-draught gunboats at a respectful distance.

We could not have held out very long against
such odds, for the enemy's shells were raking us
fore and aft and killing and wounding our men at
the guns, but the " St. Lawrence " at last got afloat
and came up under tow of a tugboat, making short
work with the little gunboats, which speedily fled
out of her range.

Fortunately for us, night was approaching, and by seven o'clock the pilots of the "Virginia" decided that it was no longer safe to maneuver her in the channel, so she ironically fired a good-night shot and steamed off to anchor at Craney Island, leaving behind her perhaps the most disheartened naval squadron that ever floated the stars and stripes.

CHAPTER XV.

IRON AGAINST IRON.

IT has often been said that the Rebellion reached its high water mark when Pickett's division delivered its gallant charge at Gettysburg, but it is a question, perhaps, if the Confederacy was not nearer a crowning success on the first night of the Hampton Roads fight than at any other period of its career.

So far as human foresight could reach, nothing stood in the way of the destruction of the rest of the Federal fleet on the morrow. Wherever the telegraph reached in the Confederacy the greatest exultation prevailed, and in many places public thanksgiving services were held then and on the following Sunday morning.

Victory meant the opening of the Chesapeake and James Rivers, the raising of the blockade, the placing of Washington and, perhaps, the great commercial cities of the north under tribute, and, best of all, the recognition of belligerent rights by the nations of Europe. Truly, the Confederacy had

cause for thanksgiving, if ever, on that Saturday
night.

All over the North, on the contrary, was gloom
and despondency, and in Northern churches prayers
were offered for succor where none seemed possible. But all these conditions were destined to a
most unexpected reversal.

Worn out with excitement, and waiting for the
expected explosion of the still burning "Congress,"
I had thrown myself down beside an ammunition
chest on deck and gone fast asleep, when somebody fell over me about midnight, and I awoke to
the consciousness of an unusual bustle and excitement. Somewhat dazed, I could not at first make
out what was going on, but presently pulled myself together, and, climbing upon the hammock
netting, looked down upon a nondescript craft just
making fast alongside of us.

She shone ruby red in the light of the burning
frigate, little more than a mile distant, and active,
gnomelike figures sprang about her low-lying
deck or climbed over a queer hatbox-looking
structure amidships. At that time neither pictures
nor descriptions had made her appearance familiar
to the public, and "Jacky" himself knew nothing
whatever about her.

However, serious as the situation was, he hung

over the rail and made his jokes at her till one
o'clock, when the "Congress" blew up, and left the
broad bay in darkness. All night long the "Monitor" men, already weary with a two days' fight
for life on the ocean, were busy preparing for the
morrow's battle.

Here, at least, was a new element in the fight,
and "Jacky's" spirits rallied wonderfully, believ-
ing religiously in the traditional luck of the
American navy.

We did not know then how four months after
the reconstruction of the "Virginia" was fairly
begun, plans for the "Monitor," the invention of John
Ericsson, had been somewhat doubtfully adopted
by the Government as an experiment, — how work
had been pushed to the uttermost, and how, at last,
she had been been hurried off to sea without even
a trial trip, and with a crew to whom her machinery was wholly new and the mechanical devices
for loading her heavy guns quite unfamiliar.

It is a singular fact that this was also true of her
destined antagonist. The "Virginia" was hardly
well rid of her mechanics when she was sent into
action. Her crew was untrained and undisciplined,
some of them being artillery-men detailed from the
army for this service. Another curious coinci-
dence is that both Captain Buchanan and Lieuten-

ant Worden were on the sick list when the fight
began, and both were wounded and disabled before
it was over.

The little " Monitor," never having been tried at
sea, being the first of her type that was ever set
afloat, was more of an experiment even than the
" Virginia," which had some prototypes, at least,
in the French navy. Of the perilous voyage of
the " Monitor " from New York to Hampton Roads
no details need here be given, but as she passed
in between the Virginia Capes her anxious and
exhausted crew heard the booming of heavy guns,
and rightly guessed that the fight was already on.
In the smooth water of the lower Chesapeake she
was soon making good time toward the scene of
action, where she arrived shortly after dark.

Her orders were to proceed immediately to
Washington to complete her equipment and be on
hand to defend the capitol, but, as fortunately
happens sometimes, Lieutenant Worden was one
who was ready to disobey orders when he saw
good reason for it. Accordingly, he stayed in
Hampton Roads and tied up alongside the " Minnesota," as I have related.

Sunday morning dawned as bright and beautiful
as the Saturday that preceded it, and both sides
were early awake in anticipation of the events

that were to follow. Everybody in the eastern counties who could reach a point commanding a view of Hampton Roads came to witness the final destruction of the Yankee fleet. The Federals had not been idle during the night, and everything that ingenuity could devise had been done to strengthen the defenses on sea and land in the desperate hope that some lucky shot might find a weak point in the hitherto invulnerable foe.

After giving her men time to get their breakfast comfortably, the "Virginia" and her consorts got under way, and came down the river in leisurely fashion to resume the work of devastation so satisfactorily begun the day before. Her first intended victim was the "Minnesota," which still hung fast on Hampton Bar, where her treacherous pilot had laid her up for the convenience of his rebel friends.

While still a mile away, she fired a shot from her bow rifle which fairly hulled us, and served effectually as a foretaste of what was to follow at closer quarters. But it was the signal, too, for the little "Monitor" to steam out from behind her consort and head direct for her formidable adversary. For the first time in the world's history, two heavily armed and heavily armored steamships were about to meet in action!

We boys who hung in the "Minnesota's" rigging

and watched the fight from a distance little guessed what it all meant. But it was, at least, better fun than being knocked to pieces after yesterday's fashion without half a chance of being able to hit back.

The "Virginia" fired away as rapidly as possible with her big Brooke rifle, but the low, black, revolving turret was not so easy to hit as the broadside of a wooden frigate, and her gunners were perhaps somewhat disconcerted by this apparition that looked, as they afterwards said, "like a Yankee cheese box on a raft." At any rate, they did not hit her, and the "Monitor" reserved her fire until she could get to very close quarters.

When nearly alongside she delivered her two eleven-inch solid shot from the turret guns with a weight of concussion that made the "Virginia" shiver, though it did not pierce her armor. Almost at the same moment, having now come within close range of the broadside guns, a heavy shell struck the "Monitor's" turret; it glanced harmlessly off, though the entire gun crew felt the shock and looked around in anxiety to see what the effect would be. Nothing happened. The turret was as stanch as ever, and when the engineer turned his crank the heavy structure revolved as easily as before. Anxiety on this point was relieved.

The ironclads now turned and repassed one another at even closer quarters. The " Virginia " making the most of her ten guns and numerous crew, and firing as rapidly as she could; the " Monitor," with her small crew and only two guns, responded deliberately, firing at intervals of about seven minutes. Owing to her lighter draught and greater ease in handling, she could, to a considerable extent, choose her own position and so at times gain a temporary advantage. Once she caught the " Virginia " in a position where none of her guns could be brought to bear, and again she tried to ram the " Virginia's " steering gear, but missed it by a few feet. So the mighty duel went on. And we of the wooden ships could only watch its progress with increasing anxiety, but, upon the whole, with growing confidence in our little champion.

Lieutenant Jones at length made up his mind that there was no use in wasting powder against a solid iron turret, so he decided to turn his attention again to ships that he could sink. The " Minnesota " was nearest at hand, and, slowly turning her huge bulk, the " Virginia " bore down upon us. It was her turn now to get aground, but after a little manuevering she came within range, and we opened upon her, giving her broadside after broadside, with no more effect than if our solid shot had been so many Dutch cheeses.

The enemy's shells speedily set us on fire and threatened to reduce us to a wreck in short order. It looked as though the tables were to be turned again. But while we were working our guns to the best of our ability the little "Monitor" came up between us, and was at him again, and would not let him alone. He found the shot of the size that she carried could not be ignored, so the duel was resumed.

Once the "Monitor" had to run away into shoal water while she hoisted a fresh supply of ammunition into her turret, and all the spectators thought that the game was up. But in fifteen minutes she was back again, saucy and full of fight as ever, and the "Virginia" began to think that she had the worst of the bargain. Having failed to make any impression upon the turret, it occurred to Lieutenant Jones to turn his guns upon the pilot house, or "conning tower," as it would now be called.

The first shell exploded against it just as Lieutenant Worden was looking through a narrow sight-hole. His eyes were blinded by the burning powder, and he was for the moment totally disabled. He managed, however, to give the order to sheer off, thinking that the conning tower had been destroyed, and tottered down the ladder, where he was found almost insensible by Lieutenant Green, who was at once called to take command.

The wounded officer was left in charge of Surgeon Logue, and the fight continued. During the few minutes of confusion following Worden's wound the "Monitor" had been without a helm, and as her engines were still working she had taken her way into shoal water. When Lieutenant Green got her in hand again the "Virginia" was heading for Norfolk, and, although he followed and gave her three or four parting shots, she had apparently had enough of it, and never again ventured to face the "Monitor's" guns. She was destroyed some two months afterward by her own crew to prevent her falling into the hands of the Federals.

Practically, neither ship was seriously harmed by this protracted encounter; each was struck many times, and the "Virginia" had pretty much everything swept away that did not belong to her solid armor. Her smoke-stack was so damaged that her engines could not be made to work as well as usual. While her injuries were not of a permanent character, it is a fact that she went into dry dock at Norfolk, and was for a month undergoing extensive repairs and improvements. The

" Monitor's " injuries, on the contrary, were so
slight that her own crew did all that was necessary,
and had her in fighting trim within a few hours after
recovering from their extraordinary exertions.

The fact is that after this engagement both the
Confederates and the Federal Governments were
afraid to risk another like it. The Federals assembled a large fleet in Hampton Roads, the " Monitor " being still their only ironclad, and instructions
were given to the flag officer, Commodore Golds-
boro, to sacrifice his entire wooden fleet before
allowing the " Monitor " to go into action.

This policy was probably the wisest that could
have been adopted, but it was very unpopular in
the fleet, and especially on board the " Monitor "
herself, whose crew longed to settle the question of
superiority once for all. Once or twice more the
" Virginia " ran out from Norfolk, and practically
dared the Federals to come on, but, while we were
all ready to act on the defensive, our instructions
were not to open the attack. At the time we all
thought the policy was cowardly, and were corre-
spondingly indignant. But the fact that in two
months the " Virginia " was rendered forever
harmless without the loss of a single life justifies
the policy of inaction in the light of history.

It only remains to say that after the " Virginia "

had thus been disposed of, the "Monitor" rested on her laurels at Hampton Roads until December, 1862, when she was ordered South, was caught in a gale off Cape Hatteras, and foundered at sea, carrying down with her sixteen of her sixty-five men.

Within the year, therefore, these two ships, which in an encounter of a few hours' duration turned topsy-turvy the naval architecture of the world, lay at the bottom of the sea together. Meanwhile, other monitors and other casemated ironclads were building, and the superiority of types was to be settled in other waters.

But Jack Benson is "overrunning his reckoning," as the best of navigators sometimes do. In other words, his log in its revised form is outgrowing the notes hastily penciled on all sorts and conditions of paper when he was "afore the mast." At the end of a sizable volume he is not yet half way through with his record, and has been barely a year in the service. He sees nothing for it, therefore, but to go on and spin his yarn through another book, to be called, "A Medal of Honor Man."

END.